THE HOUSE AT THE EDGE OF MAGIC

THE HOUSE AT THE EDGE OF MAGIC

Amy Sparkes

WALKER
BOOKS

First published 2021 by Walker Books Ltd
87 Vauxhall Walk, London SE11 5HJ

6 8 10 9 7 5

Text © 2021 Amy Sparkes
Cover and interior illustration © 2021 Ben Mantle

The right of Amy Sparkes to be identified as author of
this work has been asserted by her in accordance with
the Copyright, Designs and Patents Act 1988

This book has been typeset in Berkeley Oldstyle

Printed and bound in Great Britain by CPI Group (UK) Ltd

British Library Cataloguing in Publication Data:
a catalogue record for this book
is available from the British Library

ISBN 978-1-4063-9531-0

www.walker.co.uk

The author will donate 5% of her
royalties for this book to ICP Support
www.icpsupport.org
Reg. charity number: 1146449

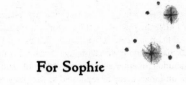

For Sophie

To Whoever Reads This Note,

My name is Nine and I need you to do me a favour.

Go down Whinney's Passage until you reach the tumbledown terrace. Knock on the third door and say, "No strawberries today".

Tell Pockets that Nine sent you. Tell the old weasel-faced devil he will never see me again. Why? Because he's wrong – sometimes life does bring you strawberries. Sometimes you are a whisper away from magic without even realising it.

And that's exactly what happened to me.

Nine

CHAPTER 1

Nine crouched down behind the stacked fish crates at the bustling market. *Dead fish always look so surprised*, she thought. *Surprised to be dead? Surprised to be caught?* Well, no one would surprise Nine, anyway. She had no intention of being caught, or of dying, thank you very much. Even though she ran the risk of both every day of her life.

Nine brushed her fingertips against the empty satchel slung across her body. It wouldn't be empty for long.

Focus.

She closed her eyes for a heartbeat, then opened them again. Just like a cat: sighting her prey, stalking it quietly, pouncing at the right moment. But instead of bringing a mouse back to her owner, Nine was after a different type of gift.

She was falling out of favour with Pockets, the old gang-master. She needed to prove herself to him. Prove she was worth the roof over her head and the pathetic amount of food the old devil gave her each day. And this was her opportunity.

Everyone was busy at the market, moving and chatting. It was the perfect place for a pounce. Barrows rattled, traders shouted, wagons rolled. A shawl-wrapped fishwife was at the far end of her stall, yelling to the crowd about the Catch of the Day, which, as far as Nine was concerned, was just an extra-large, extra-surprised-looking fish. Nine ducked down behind the crates and peered around. A horse and cart clattered over the cobbles, obscuring her view. When it passed, she smiled.

Her prey. A young lady stood with her back to Nine. She guessed, by her height and build, that the lady was only a few years older than herself, but she was beautifully dressed. She had a puffed-out scarlet dress and, more importantly, a fancy, beaded handbag.

Nine's senses were on alert. Her muscles tensed. She moved into position, clenched her fists, stretched her fingers – her pre-pounce ritual.

The scarlet lady was heading for the fabric shop across the street. Perfect. When she went to open the door – that moment of distraction – Nine would crash into her and snatch the bag.

She was on in *three*...

Oh, she loved the thrill.

Two...

Focus on the prey.

One...

The young lady was nearly at the door...

Go! Nine sprinted over the cobbles, aiming for her prize—

THWACK. Nine ran straight into her, clasped the bag—

The shopkeeper opened the door right at that moment and his eyes fell on Nine and her outstretched hand. *No!* This was not good. Nine released the handbag. This was *definitely* not good. The scarlet-dress lady shrieked and stumbled backwards.

With a flash of panic, Nine dashed back towards the fish baskets. She could duck and weave through the crates and—

"HEY!"

Nine gasped as two large hands slammed down on her shoulders.

"I saw that, missy. What's your game?" growled the shopkeeper in a deep voice.

"It's called 'catch'," said Nine. Then she twisted around, grabbed the Catch of the Day and threw it at his face. The shopkeeper staggered backwards, looking even more surprised than the fish. Nine shoved over the piled-up fish crates as hard as she could – dead fish oozing like spilled guts across the street – and the shopkeeper crashed into the stall. Nine took a moment to appreciate the fishwife pounding him with a prize lobster, then ran through the streets, dodging people, horses, the huge steaming piles of—

Squelch. Nine stopped, looked down at her filth-caked shoe and wrinkled her nose.

"Oi!" Looking back, she saw the lobster-beaten shopkeeper running towards her. She huffed, then bolted as fast as she could through the market. She needed to disappear – to find protective walls to hide behind until he gave up the chase. Nine darted past shop windows and houses, longing for a glimpse of the one place she could go, the one place where she would always be safe.

Ah! And there it was! Her muscles relaxed just a little. The tall, somewhat derelict building was the safest place in the world. Two of its windows were now boarded up, roof tiles were missing, but its faded, peeling blue door was ajar and waiting.

Nine quickly glanced over her shoulder, and saw the shopkeeper still pushing past people and dodging stray dogs. A tiny smile escaped her, and Nine pushed open the door and slipped inside the library. The hinge squeaked as she closed the door behind her.

Shhh. She mustn't be heard. Mustn't be seen. While she was here she would creep in, snatch a book and leave unnoticed. It was good practice, after all.

A damp, musty smell hung in the air. A handful of ladies and gentlemen were dotted around the silent room, flicking through books and magazines, their backs towards her. No sign of the librarian. So far, so good.

Nine stepped forward. A floorboard creaked. She held her breath. Nothing.

She crept towards her favourite, but half-empty, shelf: mystery tales. Stories where answers were hidden and secrets unravelled and where, perhaps, for a moment, anything was possible. She trailed her fingertips across the soft, dark binding of the books as she passed.

She loved books. One of the older thieflings had taught her to read before he'd flown the Nest. He was the only one in the Nest who had treated Nine as a person, rather than the muck now smeared on her shoe. Nine was so grateful. Inside every book was a world: a world to which she could escape.

Her fingers stopped at a brown spine with gold lettering. *The Mystery of Wolven Moor* by Horatio Piddlewick. She stretched her fingers around the book, eased it out gently, silently and—

"Caught you," whispered a man's voice in her ear.

Nine's heart leapt into her mouth, her fingers fumbled at the book and it fell towards the floor. A hand shot out and caught it.

Nine put her hands on her hips and whirled around to face a ginger-haired librarian, who stood tall and proud. "What?! No! I was silent as the grave, Mr Downes!"

The librarian's eyes twinkled joyously behind his horn-rimmed spectacles as he waggled a finger. "Ah, the floorboard creaked." Nine rolled her eyes as Mr Downes reached inside his jacket pocket and pulled out a small notebook. He tucked the library book under his arm and turned to a heavily marked page in the notebook. "I believe the score is ... yes, twelve points to me, five to you." He beamed at Nine, then frowned suddenly and wrinkled his nose. "What *is* that smell?"

Nine tucked her filth-caked shoe behind her other leg. "Can't smell anything."

"Hmmm," said Mr Downes, twisting his mouth

to one side. He untucked the book and glanced at the cover. "*The Mystery of Wolven Moor*?"

"I've read it three times already. You really need to get some new books."

The joyful look in the librarian's eyes faded away and worry lined his face. "You know the library cannot buy new books. There's not even enough to repair the building. It's a miracle we're still open!"

"Well, then," said Nine quietly, snatching the book back and marching for the front door. "This one will have to do."

"Nine," hissed Mr Downes as he scurried along beside her, "must I keep reminding you? Without a guardian's signature and a disclosed address, you cannot have an account, and if you do not have an account, you are *not* permitted to borrow books from this library."

"It's for a friend."

"And this *friend*, I presume, also does not have an account and is not permitted to—"

Nine stopped just before she reached the front door. "You going to let me take it or not?"

Mr Downes looked at Nine and raised a gingery eyebrow. "One week."

Nine tucked the book into her satchel, gave the librarian a wink and walked out the door, smiling at the noisy, exasperated sigh from Mr Downes as she left.

CHAPTER 2

As she stepped outside a grey-bearded man, staring down at the ground, almost walked into her. A protest was on the tip of her tongue, but Nine held it back, watching as he disappeared into the pawn shop across the road. Moments later he reappeared with a spring in his step and, Nine reckoned, a good deal richer.

She kicked herself for not grabbing whatever valuable thing he'd been carrying before he went in. Pockets would have been pleased with her, for once. What had the man pawned? A family heirloom, perhaps? She thought of her most treasured possession – a little, worthless, silvery music box – the only thing in the world that was truly hers. At least it was only on Pockets' shelf and not in a pawn shop window.

Pockets. *Focus.*

Back to the market she went, her hunter's eyes searching for the perfect gift for the old man. The market was beginning to wind down for the day: the traders were shifting crates and loading carts as the last customers milled around the street. There was the young lady in scarlet again, clutching her little beaded bag – that lovely, unusual bag. What treasures were inside? Gold? Jewellery? Nine smiled. A second chance was a rare gift. This time she wouldn't mess it up. This time she would show the old devil how good she really was.

Just like a cat: sighting her prey, stalking it quietly, pouncing at the right moment. Nine moved into position, clenched her fists, stretched her fingers.

She was on in *three*…

Oh, she hated her life.

Two…

But she loved this thrill.

One…

Focus on the prey.

And – *GO!*

She dashed for the scarlet lady and grabbed her handbag, closing her fingers around the silky, expensive strap. But the lady held tight – she was ready this time.

Unfamiliar voices shouted.

"Oi!"

"Hey, you!"

Nine panicked and tugged. This really was turning into a rotten day.

Something like a small, dark ornament flew out from the bag and tumbled across the cobbles. Nine saw her chance – she released her grip, grabbed the object from the ground and ran.

Shouts and curses rang out behind her, but Nine only had eyes and ears for what was ahead. She sprinted over the cobbles, her satchel bouncing on her hip. She darted between carts, people—

"Thief!" shouted an angry voice behind her.

She glanced over her shoulder as she ran.

A ruddy-cheeked butcher with a blood-stained apron was only a stone's throw away. In a second he'd be right on top of—

THUD. She collided with a large barrel rolled by a lanky boy. The ground fell away from her feet as she flew over the barrel and crash-landed on the cobbles on the other side. Her left hand instinctively opened with the blow and the little dark object went spinning away.

Sprawled on the ground, Nine's eyes searched desperately for her prize. There – on the stones, just within reach. Nine stretched out her fingers…

The lanky boy swore at her and rolled the barrel on, accidentally kicking the object farther away. Nine watched as it skipped across the cobbles, coming to rest between the hooves of a restless horse.

"Oi, you!" came the butcher's voice. Nine scowled. The man was nearly on her. She glanced at the prize beneath the horse. Definitely some kind of ornament, sure to be valuable. She would *not* lose this. The blood-stained apron filled her

vision, a hand extended to grab her—

Nine rolled out of reach and scrabbled to her feet. She dashed towards the horse and cart, the butcher right behind her.

His angry fingers clawed at her and Nine threw herself to the ground, hearing her jacket tear as she twisted out of his grasp. She rolled between the horse's stamping hooves, snatching the ornament as she went. "Got you!" she whispered.

Nine stood up with the horse and cart safely between her and the butcher. As he turned to run around the horse, Nine stuffed the ornament into her satchel and headed for the nearest alley.

The more she twisted and turned through the maze of narrow streets, the quieter the noise from the market. The shouts of the butcher were faint and infrequent now. Chest aching, she slowed to a walk until she reached a lifeless, dead-end alley. High, brick walls with occasional gates marked the back yards of houses on each side.

Not the sort of place a person would, or probably should, linger.

Nine promised herself a moment to catch her breath, then she'd head back to Pockets. To show the old devil exactly what she was worth.

She sat on the ground, reached into her satchel for the valuable ornament and pulled out her prize...

A house.

A house? Small enough to sit in the palm of her hand; like a dolls' house from a dolls' house – but stranger. Its four narrow storeys were dotted with tiny windows and odd corners, that jutted out here and there. Tall, round towers capped with pointy spires stood on both sides. There was a slightly wonky chimney on top of a tiled roof and, at the bottom, a double-fronted blue door with a tiny doorknocker.

Nine stroked the door wistfully. A house. A home. What would it be like to live in a house, instead of Pockets' stinking Nest? She hooked her grubby little finger under the miniscule doorknocker ring, then let it fall back on the door. It made the tiniest little tap.

"Nobody's home," she said softly as she stood up. The uproar in the market would have died down now. She could probably head back to—

A tingling, buzzing feeling tickled Nine's palm. *Odd*. She glanced down. The little house was vibrating in her hand. Nine watched as it shook more strongly, the little doorknocker now clinking against the door. She plonked it straight down on the ground and stepped backwards. The house began rocking violently from side to side. Then, with a whoosh, it started growing – growing?! – upwards and outwards.

Nine stared as the house filled every available gap in the alley, its shape contorting, lengthening and repeatedly rearranging itself to fit every inch of space. Storeys poked out above the rooftops of the other buildings until the house became an unbalanced, oddly shaped eight – nine – ten – *eleven*-storey building, surely threatening to topple over at any moment.

Nine stared in shocked silence, trying to make sense of what had happened. Her eyes tracked the house from the blue front door with its not-so-tiny doorknocker right in front of her, up through the eleven wonky, squished-up storeys, all the way to the top.

The house was a copy of the little ornament, but now with new higgledy-piggledy floors and windows. Something strangely stump-like was poking out oddly from the side of the roof. It was still shaking from side to side until there was a little *pop!* and a wonky chimney shot up.

"What the—?" began Nine, but she didn't get any further. At that moment the front door opened. And there, framed by the doorway, stood a huge, ugly creature – like a cross between a walrus and a tree trunk – head and shoulders above the tallest man and twice as wide. It had bark-like grey skin, a ropey tail dangling between its legs, big yellow eyes, two tusk-like teeth…

And was wearing a white, frilly apron with a feather duster tucked into the side.

"Wh—?" said Nine, staring at the creature. Her legs had apparently forgotten how to move.

"You late," rumbled the thing. "We waiting."

And with a large, rough hand, it grabbed Nine by the collar, pulled her inside and slammed the door behind her.

CHAPTER 3

The creature gave a huge wonky, tusky grin as it plonked her, gently, on the floor. Nine immediately brought her fists up. She wasn't going down without a fight. The thing patted her head awkwardly. Nine lowered her fists slightly, more out of surprise than anything else. She hated being surprised.

"Good … dog ," the thing said, picking her up again, this time by the jacket, and looking rather confused.

"I am not!" Nine retorted, thrashing her legs wildly. "I'm not a dog, I'm a girl. And I'm definitely not good. Now leave me alone!"

"You lady?" The thing frowned and peered

closer. Standing with its back to the front door, it looked even more confused.

Nine stood as tall as she could and thought about her wild, black hair and her ragged, stained trousers. "Yes," she said defiantly. "Sort of."

The thing tilted its head, as if it was trying to understand what exactly it had just met. Nine knew she couldn't possibly understand what exactly *she* had just met. This couldn't be real. Maybe she had hit her head on the cobbles when she fell...? And this was a strange dream which her cobble-bumped brain was making up...? If it *was* a dream, it was rapidly heading towards a nightmare.

Nine glanced quickly around – she had to make her plan of escape. She was standing in a dark, plum-coloured hallway lit by a candelabra dangling from the ceiling and facing a dark, gloomy staircase.

In the house which had just popped up...

It couldn't be real.

The thing that was blocking the door, though, did look very real – and very big.

Focus. Escape.

What about windows? No ... there were no windows. Which was odd, because there were definitely windows on the outside. Instead the walls were lined with heavy-framed portraits of important-looking people, hung crookedly around the hallway and up the stairs. They all seemed to share the same slightly flared nostrils. A wooden cabinet with glass doors and many trophies stood between two doorways.

A blue and white coat of arms was mounted on one side of the front door, showing something like two sticks crossed above a large toad. On the other side was a hexagonal clock with fifteen numbers instead of twelve. It had four sword-shaped hands all pointing to '15' at the top.

Wait. 15? Why would it—?

The creature took a step towards Nine, bringing her focus back.

"Don't you reckon on eating me," she said, raising her fists again. "I tell you now, I'm all bone."

"Eat lady? *Eat lady*?" boomed the thing. It clutched its large, apron-covered belly and began to laugh a terrible laugh – a sound like two boulders being rubbed together the wrong way. Nine stared defiantly at the creature, feeling glad it couldn't hear how fast her heart was beating. She glanced sideways and saw a brass candlestick sitting on a tall, spindly legged table.

"Stay back!" she warned in a shaky voice. She grabbed the candlestick and raised her arm, ready to hurl it at the creature. "Not that you can eat me anyway, since you're *not real*!"

"EAT LADY!" guffawed the creature again.

"Naturally, Eric would do no such thing," said a calm, well-spoken voice from the staircase. "He's a vegetarian, as the fragrance of the air so thoughtfully reminds us every day. I assure you, Madam, the smell is very, *very* real."

Nine looked round to see a tall boy coming down the plum-carpeted stairs. He had auburn curly hair, which puffed out from underneath his pointed indigo hat, and the same flared-nostril nose as the portraits. He wore a long, star-speckled, indigo gown, which flowed around him as he moved. Although the boy looked only a few years older than herself, there was something rather … *ancient* about him.

"But, what…?" began Nine, then watched as the boy made his way down the dark staircase. "Who…?" She looked at the apparently very real thing called Eric. "Why…?"

"I am Flabberghast. High Wizard, Chair of the Tea Tasters Committee, World Hopscotch Champion 1835," he said, holding his head high. Then he stumbled down the last couple of steps. "Blasted gown," he muttered, staggering next to the tusky beast. "Eric, would you be so kind?"

The creature called Eric grinned and reached out a thick arm towards the wizard. With a quick movement he tore the gown away, revealing what looked like indigo pyjamas and purple, fluffy slippers underneath. Eric threw the gown towards an empty umbrella stand in the corner of the hall. Nine gasped as a blue arm zoomed up from inside it, caught the cloak, then disappeared back into the stand taking the cloak with it.

"Wretched gown. Only wear it for visitors, really. Plays havoc with one's hopscotch practice."

"Hopscotch?" Nine said incredulously.

Something fast-moving on the staircase caught Nine's eye. What appeared to be a wooden spoon with a face – and spindly arms and legs – slid down the bannister. It was wearing a kilt and brandishing a sword. The spoon whooshed off the end of the bannister and landed by Nine's feet.

"About time, lassie!" it declared. "What took you so long?"

"You talk," was all Nine managed. "That's … incredible."

"Trust me," said Flabberghast, "the novelty does wear off." He cleared his throat. "This is Dr Spoon, and—"

"Dr Spoon? That's an odd name," said Nine.

"Oh, aye?" said the spoon, pointing the sword at her. "And yours?"

"Nine."

The spoon raised an eyebrow. "We'll call it a draw."

Flabberghast cleared his throat irritably. "And Eric, our troll housekeeper."

"Hello, lady," said Eric, waving at her.

"Troll," Nine said weakly, "housekeeper." Surely those words didn't belong next to each other?

"Yes, yes, troll housekeeper," said Flabberghast impatiently. He put a hand up to his mouth and whispered to Nine, "Not a very good one. Never eat the pancakes."

"Pancakes?" Nine stared at them all and blinked. They couldn't be here, talking to her about pancakes. *None of this was real.* Was it?

Nine swallowed hard and faced the truth: even with all the books she read, she could not have made this up. So if this *was* real, and there truly *was* a housekeeping troll, a sword-waving spoon and a hopscotching wizard, then it almost certainly wasn't wise to hang around.

"Well… This has been nice," she said, trying to sound like this sort of thing happened every day, "but I really can't stay." She patted her satchel loudly to drown out the heartbeat thumping in her ears. "You know, places to go, people to rob… And, thanks to you, I need to find someone a new present because *you* seem to be living in the old one." She strutted towards the front door trying not to show the wobble in her legs.

Before she'd made it even a few steps the wizard dashed in front of the door, blocking her way. The spoon leapt up onto Nine's shoulder and held the blade of his little sword against her throat. She gasped.

"So," said Flabberghast fixing his eyes on Nine, "there's good news and there's bad news." He steepled his fingers together. "Which do you want first?"

CHAPTER 4

Nine felt a rising sense of panic in her chest. She grabbed a quick, shallow breath. As strange – as terrible – as this all was, she *had* to stay calm.

"Fine. The bad news?" she said. "Apart from the fact there's a wooden spoon about to kill me."

"Oh, that's not news. That's entirely to be expected, Madam," said the wizard, as Nine raised an eyebrow. "No, the bad news is that this house is under a curse. We cannot even step outside."

Nine gave a puzzled frown, but only for a moment. After all, considering everything that had happened in the last ten minutes, was a cursed house so unbelievable? "And the good news?"

Flabberghast clapped his hands together childishly. "*You* are the one to break it. Oh, we have been waiting for you for a very long time. The one who knocks on the door!"

The wizard and the troll grinned at her. Big, wide, fixed grins...

Nine thought quickly. They needed her. So ... surely, they wouldn't hurt her. She only hoped they'd remembered to tell the spoon that bit of information. *Remembered to tell the spoon?* Why was she even thinking this? No. This was ridiculous. She threw her hands up in the air.

"Everything about this is madness! Everything about *you* is madness!" She waved her hand at the spoon. "And is this really how you treat your guests?"

Flabberghast gave a little, nervous laugh then glared at the spoon and gestured at him to lower his sword. The spoon huffed loudly, muttered something about incompetent wizards and jumped down from Nine's shoulder.

"That's better," Nine said, hoping she sounded calm and in control, because she really wasn't – not any more. "Yes, I can fix your curse. Watch this."

She walked towards the wizard and troll, who exchanged nervous glances before stepping aside. Heart thumping, Nine grabbed the door handle, yanked open the door and stepped outside onto the uneven cobbles.

"Outside. See? Not difficult. Now, if you'll excuse me, I'll be off." She took a step away from the house—

"NO!" The utter desperation in their voices stopped Nine in her tracks. She turned around slowly to look at them. The troll was wringing his tufty-ended tail, the wizard was wringing his hands, and the spoon looked like he wanted to wring her neck.

The wizard held up his hands in surrender. "Just … step back inside, Madam," he said carefully. "You can leave the door open and I will demonstrate *exactly* what the matter is."

Slowly, Nine stepped back inside the house, eyeing the wizard warily as she did so. She could always run for it if she needed to.

The spoon hastily hopped halfway up the

staircase before turning around to watch. He clung to his kilt and looked nervous. Nine moved next to Eric, who shook his head sadly and slowly. He leaned forwards and stretched out his arms.

"Wh-what are you doing?" hissed Nine.

"Eric catch," said Eric.

"Catch?" said Nine. "Catch what?"

"Madam," said the boy sharply, "observe." He rolled up his indigo sleeves, took a deep breath and went to take a step outside.

There was a BOOM – a soundless BOOM. More a feeling of having *been* BOOMed. A ripple of energy washed over Nine and her satchel flapped up and hit her on the nose. The candelabra flickered and went out, and the wizard was thrown backwards, landing in the arms of the troll. He scrambled back down to the floor and smoothed his pyjamas indignantly. The candelabra relit itself with a gentle whoosh.

Nine opened her mouth to speak but had no words.

"You see, Madam," Flabberghast snapped.

"The indignity of it! The sheer spite! I thoroughly dislike flying in all its forms."

"Lady help?" said Eric, with a pleading look in his eyes.

"Aye," said the spoon, looking Nine up and down. "Desperate times call for desperate measures."

Nine shuffled uncomfortably. "Help? Well … don't you have a back door?"

"Oh, if *only* we'd thought of that!" hissed the wizard through clenched teeth. "Of course we have a back door. The problem is the cursemaker thought of that, too…"

Flabberghast shepherded Nine down the hallway and the spoon jumped from the bannister onto Eric's shoulder as the troll followed. As Nine passed the staircase on the left, she noticed the cupboard under the stairs had a sign pinned on it: NEVER OPEN THIS DOOR. There were several rooms on the right-hand side, which was odd. Nine was sure the layout of the house on the inside didn't match the squashed-up, eleven-storeyed house on the outside.

Nine tried to peer inside the dark rooms as she passed – she could have sworn one of them was whispering and had purple sparks flying around inside – but Flabberghast quickly moved her along and into the kitchen at the hallway's end.

Nine glanced around, keen to be aware of her surroundings in case things turned bad, which she assumed was quite possible in the company of a long-tusked troll and a clearly agitated – if not entirely unbalanced – wizard.

The kitchen was filled with random cupboards of all sizes, with a back door on the far wall. A tall hat stand was next to an arched, wooden door on the right-hand wall. On the left was a crockery-filled dresser and a large bricked fireplace with a black cauldron suspended above it. In the middle sat a wooden table and three elaborately carved wooden chairs, with which Nine could probably do a fair amount of damage, if she needed to. She should surely, at least, be a match for a wooden spoon.

Near the arched door, a slimy orange drip plopped noisily into a bucket. Nine looked up to see a damp patch on the ceiling. She opened her mouth, then decided that some questions were best left unasked.

Apart from that the kitchen looked normal enough. But then, the umbrella stand at the front door had looked normal enough before a blue arm had zoomed out of it...

"Eric," The wizard stood by the table. "If you would be so kind."

The troll's long toenails scratched along the brick-paved floor as he lolloped towards the back door. He turned and beckoned her. Slowly, Nine followed him.

"Lady open," Eric said as the spoon pointed his sword at her, then at the door.

Nine put her hand on the handle, wondering when the chair-bashing should begin. But Nine had never been able to help her curiosity, which was why she found herself pulling the handle down and quickly opening the door...

CHAPTER 5

Six heavily armoured, ferocious-looking, human-ish creatures stood there, brandishing spears and jagged, black swords. They towered over Nine, were grey as slate, bug-eyed and had saliva dripping from their fangs. They roared and waved their weapons. Nine stared at them blankly for a moment, trying to make sense of anything.

Swiftly deciding this was a waste of her time, she shut the door in their faces.

Nine pressed her lips tightly together, then whirled around to face the others. "And I suppose those creatures live in your garden, day and night!" she said.

"Don't be ridiculous, Madam," scoffed Flabberghast. "Only on Tuesdays."

"Is Monday dragon, Tuesday goblin, Wednesday…" Eric said, counting on his fingers. He kept mumbling away but Nine marched back to Flabberghast.

"Well, I *can* get out of this house and that is exactly what I'm going to do." She headed for the hallway but the wizard caught her arm and spun her around to face him. He looked her up and down.

"Madam, I presume since you dress in this odd, bedraggled attire, you have very little in the way of wealth—"

"*Odd, bedraggled attire?*" protested Nine.

"—and I can offer you riches, Madam, riches beyond your imagination."

Oh. Wait. Riches? Nine narrowed her eyes, thoughtfully.

"Just so you know," she said, softening her voice a little, "my imagination is very good."

The wizard smiled and released her arm. "Come with me."

He wandered back down the hallway, stopping at a silver-painted wooden door on the left. Nine looked at Eric, who nodded enthusiastically. She walked over to Flabberghast.

"Madam," he said as he opened the door, "behold." A strange red glow from the room lit up his face.

Nine gave him a suspicious look. What was he playing at? But curiosity once more got the better of her and she peered inside. The room was no bigger than a large cupboard and suspended in the air was a red glowing ball.

"What is it?" murmured Nine.

"A jewel of immense monetary value is encased within this orb," said Flabberghast. "My inheritance from a relative I held in great esteem. People would pay a vast amount to possess it. It holds great personal value but the curse has encased it in this orb, beyond anybody's reach. See for yourself."

Nine looked at Flabberghast doubtfully, but he nodded. She edged towards the floating red ball, slowly stretching out her hand and, with the very tip of her finger, she went to touch it. A fizzing spark of red shot out with a loud hiss. Instantly Nine pulled her hand away.

"Once the curse is lifted, the imprisoned jewel will be accessible once again. Madam, it can be yours if you will break the curse which binds us."

A jewel of immense value. She could fly the Nest. Never have Pockets sneering and shoving her again. Unable to resist, Nine stared at the beautiful red ball – a thing that could transform her whole life. Then she looked at the front door, trying to decide which truly held the most appeal.

Out of the corner of her eye she saw the wizard and the troll. She turned to look at them standing side by side with wide, frozen, desperate grins on their faces, and the spoon between their legs scowling and pointing his sword towards her.

"No," she said decisively, "this is still madness. I'm leaving." She marched towards the front door.

"Nononononono!"

Flabberghast dashed ahead of her and blocked her way. Nine folded her arms. "Say you'll think about it, Madam? Come back tomorrow."

She drummed her fingers on her folded arm.

"The immeasurable wealth could transform your life! Lift you from the depths of wretched peasantry—"

"*Peasantry*?!" Nine narrowed her eyes and flung her arms by her side. "My life is perfectly fine, thank you very much. I don't need you – or anyone – to fix it. Move."

Flabberghast groaned, slumped his shoulders and moved away from the door. He stood next to the troll who patted the top of the wizard's pointy hat too hard, crumpling the point and shoving the rim down over his eyes.

Nine yanked open the door.

"Immeasurable weeeeeealth!" a voice pleaded behind her.

But Nine stepped outside onto the cobbles without so much as a BOOM, and slammed the door behind her. She took a deep breath and looked up at the wonky too-many-storeyed House towering behind her. It was, without question, the most ridiculous, most unbelievable, most definitely-not-real place she had ever been in her life, filled with the most ridiculous, most unbelievable and most definitely-not-real beings she had ever known in her life. And there was nothing that would ever make her step foot inside it again.

"PERFECTLY FINE," she called pointedly to the House, then stormed off into the dusk to the place she hated to call home.

CHAPTER 6

Nine headed through the winding streets towards a row of tumbledown terraced houses with boarded-up windows. She reached the third door and her shoulders tensed.

"*Wretched peasantry*," she muttered to herself, then pounded on the old wooden panels and said "No strawberries today!"

The door creaked open and an arm appeared in the gap and yanked Nine inside, pulling her roughly off her feet. The door slammed behind her as she regained her balance inside the dark hallway, lit only by a flickering candle. A short, grubby piece of rope dangled from the ceiling.

"Jim, I told you a million times!" she ranted at

the shadows. "DON'T TOUCH ME! Just open the blimin'—"

A hand shot out of the shadows and pulled the rope.

"—doooooooor!" The ground beneath Nine disappeared as a trapdoor swung open.

There was a smarting thump as Nine's bottom hit the metal of an old coal chute. The trapdoor slammed shut as she hurtled down in the blackness until, with a thud, she tumbled into the candle-lit Nest of a Thousand Treasures.

Heart still racing, Nine stood up on the damp cellar floor. Mary, Annie and Tom, the other thieflings, glared at her from their sackcloth beds. Nine glared back. Worn boots came softly behind her.

"You's late," grizzled Pockets' voice in her ear. His breath stank like rotten onions and month-old dead rat, which was quite possibly his last meal.

"*You're* revolting. Clean your teeth," said Nine as Pockets moved in front of her.

The old gang-master glared down at her, his white-whiskered jaw jutting to one side. "You

49

better have something pretty-shiny for Pockets' Nest," he said.

Nine thought of the scarlet lady and the failed pounce and said nothing. She knew she was falling from favour faster than a stone-stunned sparrow.

"Course she ain't," said Annie.

"She's losin' her touch," Mary added. She sucked her dirty hair and shot an evil look at Nine, who gladly returned it.

"You's useless! Pockets is kind enough to share his Nest with you!" hissed Pockets, gesturing at the cold, gloomy cellar.

"And it's such a *charming* place," said Nine. She closed her ears to Pockets' disgruntled rantings and looked around. Every nook and cranny of the room was filled with Pockets' beloved curios. Dangling from bent nails in a ceiling beam were rabbits' feet tied with string, broken lockets, once-shiny chains and a cracked – but working – pocket watch. The flickering candlelight half-revealed ugly toby jugs grinning from nooks like gargoyles.

And there, on the shelf, surrounded by old

tankards, was her little, shining music box. The only possession she had when Pockets found her...

Her oldest memory. She had been only three years old, alone and cold in a doorway. She didn't remember who left her there, or why, but she remembered the beautiful shining music box she held in her little hand. It had seemed much bigger back then.

She was sure the music box was the only reason he had taken her in. "Nine" he had called her as he'd taken her hand and dragged her away. She didn't even know her real name: she was just the ninth broken foundling to come to the Nest. And instantly her treasure – the only thing in this world that was special to her – had become his. Nine blinked away the memory and gazed at the music box longingly, her fingers aching to hold it.

The old man's voice grumbled on. "All Pockets asks is that his children bring him a gift or a bit of coin! Because, you miserable thieflings, we is on our own here!" Nine rolled her eyes and sat down on the damp floor. This could take a while.

He raised his arms, then slammed them down to his sides in defeat. "What does Pockets always say?"

"*Life don't bring you strawberries,*" Nine droned along with the other thieflings.

"Life's turned its back on you!" Pockets said, pointing at them and clambering onto a tea chest.

Oh, good grief. Not the tea chest.

"If Pockets hadn't…" muttered Nine to herself.

"If Pockets hadn't took you in," said Pockets.

"All of you'd…"

"All of you'd be on the streets by now!"

"No freedom…"

"No freedom, no life," Pockets ranted.

"Nothing," said Nine, scanning the cellar with empty eyes.

"Nothing!" Pockets finished triumphantly with an arm flourish so forceful he lost his balance and toppled off the tea chest.

Tom snorted a repressed laugh but Nine only scowled at the old man. She hated Pockets. But if he hadn't taken her in… She didn't even like to think about where she'd be now. Annoying as it was, she owed him.

Nine stomped away to her corner, hidden by a couple of rickety crates. Just as well she liked to be alone. It was better, safer, alone.

As she went, her hand lightly brushed the shelf and she snatched her little music box. It would be back before he missed it. She eased down on her thinning, frayed sackcloth bed and felt the familiar cold seep through from the stone floor. She stared at the box and felt a deep urge to turn the tiny handle. To hear that beautiful, tinkling song. That song that said once – just maybe – she was loved.

But she couldn't, not without being caught. She glared at Pockets. The only time she could hear it now was when *he* touched it. Anger prickled up and down her spine. "My life is perfectly fine," she hissed to herself, willing the words to make everything different.

She knew the words couldn't change a single thing. Yet there was something that could … the House. The curse. That glowing red ball with the jewel inside…

NO. She was never going back to that ridiculous place.

Tiredness seeped into every bone, every muscle. She pulled *The Mystery of Wolven Moor* out of her satchel, but she was in no mood for reading. She turned over on her side and pulled a thinning, grey blanket over herself, curling tight into a ball around the music box.

The heavy dullness of sleep crept over her before she could fight it. Her dreams were wild and bright. She was edging down a dark corridor towards the floating red ball, her hand outstretched. Getting closer … closer … daring to touch it, but as she stretched out her fingers, the ball exploded into red smoke and a distant, female voice began to laugh—

Nine jolted awake, the faraway voice still ringing in her head. She looked down and saw the music box still in her hand, and a shock of panic exploded in her chest. If Pockets found out it was gone… Suddenly wide awake, she pushed back the blanket and stumbled to her feet.

Nine crept silently across the cellar to the

trinket shelf. She curled her hand around her treasure for just a moment before placing it back.

"Don't you never touch that again," growled Pockets.

Nine froze for a second, then looked over to where Pockets lay sprawled on his pathetic excuse for a bed made of sheets stuffed with wool and rag and fleas. "You always was a miserable thiefling. That's the only thing worth having I ever got from you. Bring it to Pockets."

Nine clenched her jaw and snatched up the box. She took it to the old man and pushed it forcefully into his outstretched palm.

In a sudden rush of movement, he grabbed the front of her jacket and pulled her down towards him.

"It's mine now. Keep yer hands off."

Every muscle in Nine's body tensed. She stared at him fiercely, willing her eyelids not to blink, glad he couldn't hear her heart racing. Never show him weakness. Never.

She'd done that once when she was small – cried as Pockets' filthy fingers turned her little music box handle. Pockets had given her some bruises to stop her crying, to toughen her up. It had worked. She hadn't cried since.

"Pockets got plenty other thieflings to keep him happy!" hissed Pockets through blackened teeth.

"Plenty," muttered Mary from the shadows.

"He can live without a Nine. But you'll be starving on the streets in a week without a Pockets."

The old man released Nine roughly, pushing her backwards. He examined the precious box in his hand. The silvery metal gleamed. He spat on it and polished it with his grubby sleeve.

"I hate you," whispered Nine. Her hands balled into fists.

"But you stay. 'Cos you need Pockets. You all need Pockets!" He glanced around the Nest, a cold smile spreading over his life-stained face. He stared back at Nine. "Don't you?"

He slowly turned the handle of the music box and a stuttered, melancholy tinkling filled the quiet cellar. Nine swallowed hard, fists still clenched. She was powerless. The voice of a ridiculous wizard pleaded in her head. "*Immeasurable weeeeeealth!*"

She could not bear the thought of returning to that strange, strange House. But … immeasurable wealth?

No freedom, no life, nothing…

A volcano of frustration erupted inside her. Her life wasn't perfectly fine. And there was only one way to change that.

Throwing her satchel over her shoulder, Nine stormed over to another dark corner. A long piece of rope dangled from a ceiling beam. Up she scrambled, ignoring the harsh rope burning her palms, and the glares of the other thieflings. She squeezed herself through the dark hole at the top and pulled herself onto gritty floorboards.

Nine got to her feet in the darkened upstairs lobby and straightened her satchel. A hand shot out of the shadows. In a blurry rush, she was grabbed by her jacket, whirled around to face the front door, then thrown out into the street. She growled as the door slammed behind her.

It was the early morning light, Nine was certain, which made her eyes burn and prickle and threaten to water. She swallowed hard and pushed the horrible feeling away.

She hated the old man who had saved her. She hated this life. And she hated that her only way out was to return to the ridiculous House at the end of the alley.

She sighed loudly and began to walk.

CHAPTER 7

Nine marched back down the twisting lanes and back down the alley where the House stood. She passed a couple of people who seemed blissfully unaware of this strange House that had appeared from nowhere. Couldn't they see it? More magic. More ridiculous, unreasonable magic.

But Nine could see it. And she glared at the absurd, squashed-up building with its annoying turreted towers either side of the utterly stupid front door, its slightly wonky chimneypot, its pathetic windows that weren't even on the inside because they were *that* pathetic.

Chest heaving, jaw clenched, she thought of Pockets holding her beautiful music box and pummelled furiously on the front door – then gave it a kick for good measure. There was something cream and papery poking out of the black letterbox mounted on the wall next to the door. She plucked it out – a blank envelope – and stuffed it into her satchel.

As Eric opened the door, wearing that pointless feather duster tucked into his pointless white apron, a look of delight bloomed in his completely ridiculous, yellow eyes and his stupid, wonky-tusky grin. Nine had only one word for him.

"MOVE!"

She stormed inside and slammed the door behind her. She stood on the doormat in the entrance hall, every muscle tense. The troll lolloped over to the safe distance of the staircase and stood on the bottom stair. He grabbed his long, thin tail and brought it in front of his stomach. He fiddled with the tufty fur at the end of the tail, wringing it and eyeing Nine nervously.

"WHAT?" said Nine, daring the troll to so much as breathe in her direction.

"Lady sad," said Eric quietly.

For a split-second, Nine faltered and caught her breath. She shuffled uncomfortably on the doormat.

"No."

"Lady sad."

"NO!" shouted Nine as the horrible prickling feeling built up behind her eyes. She thought again of what happened last time she had cried and the anger swelled. "And stop wearing that ridiculous apron. You look ... ridiculous!"

A door clicked open on the right. "Ah, Madam," came a smooth, well-spoken voice from inside the room.

Flabberghast appeared, wearing the same hat, indigo pyjamas and fluffy purple slippers. Nine closed her eyes and took a deep, slow breath, wondering what the chances were of getting through this without breaking someone's nose.

"I thought I heard your euphonious voice."

The chances grew smaller.

"Of course, Madam, I knew you would see sense. Realise the error of your—"

"I need your floaty red ball ... thing. I need the

money, the immeasurable wealth. That's the only reason I'm here. Not for you." Nine swallowed. "For me. Let's break this curse, get that jewel and then I never want to set eyes on any of you again."

Flabberghast raised an eyebrow and cleared his throat. "As you wish, Madam. After you." He gave an awkward bow and gestured with his arm towards the kitchen.

Nine looked around for any sign of the spoon, and was relieved that there were no spindly limbs, kilts or pointy swords in sight. She had marched about halfway down the long hallway when a small explosion came from somewhere upstairs, rattling the candelabra and the trophy cabinet. Nine paused for a moment – tense, listening – then turned round to look at Flabberghast and the troll, who appeared entirely unbothered by the explosion or the smell of rotten turnip now wafting down the stairs.

Flabberghast gave a wide, unconvincing smile. "Do proceed, Madam."

Nine raised an eyebrow at him, but continued into the kitchen. She pulled out one of the carved wooden chairs at the kitchen table and flopped into it. She folded her arms and glared at the bucket collecting the orange ceiling slime, drop by drop. But slowly, very slowly, her rage began to calm.

"Perhaps some tea before we begin?" suggested Flabberghast, giving the troll a sideways glance. The troll looked doubtful and wrung his tail again. "Tea," Flabberghast repeated, more sternly.

Eric lolloped over to the dresser and began rattling some crockery. Flabberghast walked over to a shoulder-height cupboard and stroked it thoughtfully. Eric clattered a tea tray down onto the table and began unloading three delicate cups and saucers decorated with golden stars, a matching milk jug and a sugar bowl. Nine was looking back towards Flabberghast and the cupboard when she saw a small movement out of the corner of her eye.

"That sugar bowl's lid just moved," she said, snapping her attention back to the table. Slowly Nine leaned forward and lifted the slightly chipped lid open a crack. There was a little muffled explosion and a cloud of green smoke puffed over Nine's face. She froze for a moment and then slowly replaced the lid. The sooner she got out of here, the better.

Eric hung a black iron kettle over the fire. He and Flabberghast looked at each other nervously across the kitchen, then looked at Nine.

"Madam, if you'd be so kind?" Flabberghast beckoned Nine with his finger.

She hesitated, then reluctantly walked towards him. Flabberghast smiled, nodded enthusiastically and clasped his hands together. "The tea's in there. Open the cupboard." He leaned forwards and whispered. "With the handle."

Nine glared at him suspiciously and looked at the handle of the cupboard. It was made of green crystal, with many tiny, different sides. She slowly reached her hand out … then paused. She sensed something odd behind her.

She turned around to look. Flabberghast and Eric were leaning forward eagerly, though Eric was nervously twisting his tail in his hands. Nine frowned and turned back to the cupboard, touched the crystal handle and—

ZAP! A strange, tickling buzz crackled up her hand. She snatched her hand away from the handle and screamed. Her hand – in fact all of her – had suddenly sprouted brown fur.

"What the—!"

"Don't worry," sighed Flabberghast behind her. "It will go back to normal in a few seconds."

"But what just—?" she began, turning around. "Oh."

Eric was wearing a beautiful pink tutu and clutching a sparkly wand. Flabberghast had sprouted a dragon's tail and a fluffy white beard. Both of them looked bitterly disappointed. A mouse poked its head out of Flabberghast's beard, changed its mind and dashed back inside.

The wizard looked on the verge of tears. "We thought now *you* were here, there was the smallest chance we could open the tea cupboard again. It's been three years since the curse. Three years since I've had a cup of tea! I love tea."

The magic faded and all three of them returned to normal. Nine examined her hands in relief.

Then she frowned. "You mean – so, you can

never open the cupboard and if you try…"

She touched the handle.

ZAP! Nine's skin had turned blue and she had the trunk of an elephant. Her satchel grew a stripy tail. She turned around. Eric was magically suspended upside-down by one of his huge feet, his apron flapping over his face and trailing on the brick floor. Flabberghast had become an oversized yellow spotty teapot wearing his wizard's hat.

The magic faded and they returned to normal.

"You mean *every time* I—"

ZAP! Eric was a chicken with sapphire eyes. Flabberghast was gift-wrapped in turquoise ribbon. Nine had three heads.

"Something incredible—"

ZAP! Eric became a beanpole version of himself. Nine's legs turned to springs. Flabberghast was sprawled against the ceiling, facing the ground.

"Madam!" he barked. "Kindly desist!"

The magic wore off and he plummeted to the ground with a grunt. He picked himself up and Eric gave him a quick brushing-down with his feather duster. Flabberghast glared at Nine, who couldn't quite keep the smile from her lips, then went over to the table.

"Just a nice cup of tea." He slumped into a chair.

"Fine, you don't get your tea," said Nine, back to business. "That's heart-breaking, but I need that jewel. So, let's get on with it. How do I break this wretched curse?"

"Now *that*, Madam," declared Flabberghast, steepling his fingers together in a way that was now quite ominous, "is the really interesting part."

CHAPTER 8

"**O**h no," said Nine. A terrible sinking feeling hit her stomach. "You don't know, do you?" She put her hands on her hips. "You don't know!"

"Madam, I have no clue. No clue … and no tea." Flabberghast slumped forwards into a heap on the table.

Nine marched over, grabbed a handful of the boy's curly hair and lifted his head.

"Right. Tell me about this curse." She dropped his head back down then, throwing herself in the chair opposite him, she folded her arms and glared.

Flabberghast sat up and fell backwards in his chair. "There was," he sighed, "a witch—"

"Witch clever," interrupted Eric as he reached over and sadly reloaded the cups and saucers onto the tray.

"And, with good reason, mind, I had a slight disagreement with this witch."

Eric noisily stacked the crockery back into the dresser.

"As a result of this slight disagreement, she most maliciously shrank our House to a tiny size, so easily overlooked, and placed it under a terrible, terrible curse, only to be broken by one who knocks on the door."

Nine looked at the back door. "So you can't get out the back door, or the front door, open your tea cupboard—"

"The socks!" Flabberghast hissed, making Nine jump. He pushed back his chair and slammed his purple-fluffy-slipper-wearing foot onto the table. He hitched up his indigo pyjama leg to reveal a pink sock with unicorns on. He slammed his other foot onto the table and revealed a sky-blue sock with silver triangles. "The laundry basket is cursed, so regardless of how carefully you pair your socks –" his voice became strangely high-pitched – "you can never find the one that matches! Pure evil."

Nine looked at Eric, who was nodding sympathetically. "Gets worse," he said.

"And the pictures!" spluttered Flabberghast, a look of desperation on his face. He leapt to his feet and ran to the hallway. Eric lolloped after him. Nine pushed back her chair and followed them. "Look what she's done to the pictures!"

Flabberghast reached out and straightened the portrait of 'Sir Ignatius the Permanently Late (1589–1641)'. It remained straight for a hopeful two seconds before swinging back to hang crooked. Flabberghast shook his fists at the air and let out a strangled roar.

"Poor Flabby." Eric put a comforting arm around him and patted him slightly too hard.

Flabberghast huffed. "Flab-BER-GHAST."

But Eric just looked at Nine, his big yellow eyes full of pity. "Gets worse."

"She's taken the toad's tongue, so the House can't move—"

"Move? Toad? TONGUE?" frowned Nine.

"I've missed three years of Hopscotch Championships!"

"Gets worse."

"And you can never find the toilet when you need it. It was last seen disguised as a pot plant on the eighth floor—"

"And worse..." droned the troll.

"She changed Eric's cookery books into Dwarvish!" Flabberghast shook his hands in rage. "Dwarvish! An unreadable, unspeakable language! Even the dwarves gave up!" He pointed upstairs. "And the library where the books were carefully arranged, alphabetically and in categories? No matter how long I spend rearranging them, by the morning they are all jumbled up and I can't find a blasted thing!"

Flabberghast grabbed fistfuls of his curls. "Last month I found a book on transdimensional travel in the knitting section! *The knitting section*! UPSIDE DOWN! Admittedly, the library was always a little on the emotional side – *The Hopscotch Guide for Idiots* has never quite forgiven

me for accidentally dropping it down the toilet –
but I tell you this: since the curse, the library has
been in a permanently atrocious mood!"

Eric patted Flabberghast's back, sending him
stumbling forwards a step. "More worse."

"Yes. Because worst of all," said Flabberghast
darkly, "my magic has been stolen."

"Stolen?" said Nine.

She jumped as Flabberghast thrust his hands
towards her. He wiggled his fingers.

"See? Nothing!" he hissed. "We have no idea
how to break the curse. We're trapped in this
House of chaos with no freedom, no magic and
no tea!"

No freedom, no life, nothing…

Nine shook Pockets' voice from her head.

Eric lifted the bottom corner of his apron
and wiped Flabberghast's eyes. Then he covered
Flabberghast's nose with the apron. The wizard
blew heartily.

"Well, there was something in your letterbox,"
said Nine, reaching into her satchel and holding out
the crumpled blank envelope. "Maybe it's a clue?"

Flabberghast snatched it from her. As he held it in his hands, swirly scarlet writing appeared on the envelope.

'LET'S PLAY.'

"That is *not* normal," said Nine, keeping her voice oh-so-steady-and-not-at-all-panicky. "How did that just appear?"

Flabberghast gulped and looked up at Nine.

"The witch," he whispered, looking over both shoulders then taking the envelope back into the kitchen.

"Witch clever," said Eric, as he and Nine followed the wizard. Flabberghast quickly placed the envelope on the table and stared at it nervously. He gave it a little poke with his finger.

"Hello?" he whispered.

"Come on then – open it," said Nine irritably. "It's not going to bite you."

Flabberghast looked at her darkly and raised an eyebrow.

"...is it?" asked Nine.

"Who knows what bedevilled mischief lies within this envelope!"

"Eric scared."

Nine huffed loudly, snatched the envelope from the table and hastily stuffed it into Flabberghast's hand.

"Open it," she growled.

The wizard glared at her, took a sharp intake of breath through his nose, flaring his nostrils, then he turned the envelope over. Eric covered his face with his apron, then peeped with one eye. Nine clenched her fists and tensed her legs, ready for whatever was coming.

Flabberghast lifted the envelope's flap, quickly looked around, and pulled out a piece of parchment. He flinched, but nothing happened.

"Was that it then?" Nine realised she was holding her breath and let it out. Everything seemed fine.

"Everything seems fine," said Flabberghast.

WHOOMPH! A red, glowing streak, about the width and length of Nine's arm, shot out of the envelope. Nine gave a yelp as it whizzed up and down, here and there, faster than Nine could watch it: knocking Flabberghast's hat into the cauldron;

shooting over to the dresser and smashing plates and cups; twisting and whooshing around Eric's tail; sending the bucket and its orange, slimy contents all over Flabberghast; upturning the table; darting – whooshing – whizzing – smashing – whirling – left – right – up – down –

Until it came to a stop.

Nine froze. The streak was right in front of her face. It hovered in the air like some devilish giant, red tadpole. Nine tried to stare it down, though her heart was thumping in her ears.

"Madam," whispered Flabberghast, retrieving his now-dripping hat from the cauldron. "I strongly suggest you do – not – move."

Nine had no intention of moving, largely because her legs had forgotten to do so. But on hearing the wizard's voice, the red streak seemed to look in his direction, then shot down the hallway.

Releasing her breath, Nine followed the others as they dashed after the streak.

SMASH! There went the trophy cabinet, showering tiny shards of glass everywhere and sending all the trophies plummeting to the carpet. The red streak zig-zagged across the hallway at a furious pace, knocking all the portraits and the coat-of-arms by the door upside down. Then it hurtled towards the hexagonal clock mounted by the doorway and, with another strange WHOOMPH, it shot inside the clock and disappeared. For a moment, the clock face glowed red before returning to normal.

Silence. Nine, Flabberghast and Eric looked at each other, and then looked back at the clock. There was a loud *clunk*, then three of the four sword-shaped hands started whizzing around at different paces. Backwards. With another decisive *clunk* the fourth – smallest – hand moved to the 14.

"I have a most horrible feeling about this," said Flabberghast. "That clock has not been functional since the curse. Eighteen times I've been late for breakfast because of it."

Dr Spoon came sliding down the bannister, sword drawn and eyes wild. Black smudges were dotted over his face and there was a definite smell of singed wood. "Are the green-horned Minotaurs attacking again? What the devil's going on?"

"'What the devil' is right, Spoon." Flabberghast looked at him and then at the clock. "The witch."

Spoon looked grim. "Courage, laddie."

Nine looked at the crumpled-up parchment in the wizard's hand. "Is this letter going to destroy the entire House?"

"I honestly don't know," said Flabberghast. He straightened out the first page, cleared his throat nervously and began to read.

"Dearest Flabberghast, I can only assume that if you are reading this letter, then your miniscule House has been found by some poor, unsuspecting fool—"

Spoon pointed his sword at Nine. "The lass," he said. Nine frowned.

"And so, Flabberghast, the game begins!" the wizard continued. *"The curse cannot, and will not, be lifted until you say the magic words. You have until the clock strikes fifteen to find those words, speak them aloud and break the curse. If you do not, then this time your House will shrink and shrink, but will not stop. Everything and everyone inside the House will shrink and shrink and will not*

stop, until you shrink beyond reality and vanish. Then you, Flabberghast, and everyone inside that ridiculous House –" Flabberghast looked at the others with wide eyes – "*will CEASE TO EXIST.*"

CHAPTER 9

There was a sharp intake of breath from everyone in the room.

"Cease to exist?!" cried Flabberghast.

"No shrink! No vanish!"

"Read on, laddie!"

"*But I am not an unreasonable creature,*" Flabberghast continued, followed by a snort and the raise of an eyebrow. "*Obviously someone as pathetically hopeless as yourself will need all the help you can get from your ridiculous companions. Since even that may not be enough to compensate for your continuous stupidity, you will need a clue; so the magic words are…*"

He turned over the page. Then flapped it back

over again. His shoulders slumped and he covered his eyes with his hand.

"What?" said Nine, moving closer to look. She snatched the letter from him and read the bottom of the parchment. "*The magic words are…*" She turned over the page. It was blank. "And there was nothing else in the envelope?"

Flabberghast shook his head and Nine glanced up at the clock. The hands were still whizzing backwards, the shortest inching towards the 13.

"There doesn't need to be anything else!" snapped Flabberghast. "The magic words are right there!" He jabbed his finger below the final words.

Nine squinted at the blank space on the parchment and frowned. "But—"

"It's a game! The words are there! Hidden from view! Made secret!" Flabberghast wiggled his fingers wildly at the letter. "My magic could have revealed them! But she stole my magic. And I can't get my magic back until I reveal this secret. It's impossible! The witch is impossible! It's ALL impossible!"

Flabberghast snatched the parchment from Nine and shook it furiously. With a spike of fear, Nine could feel the floaty ball, the jewel, this one chance of freedom, slipping away.

"That witch is clever," said the spoon.

"SHE IS NOT CLEVER!" bellowed Flabberghast.

"Stop shouting!" shouted Nine. "That's not going to solve anything!"

"I'm not shouting, you are!"

"I. AM. NOT."

Eric whimpered and put his yellow-nailed hands over his ears. "Eric shrink!"

Nine refused to acknowledge the stab of pity that she very nearly felt. She took a deep breath and closed her eyes.

Focus. Calm. Panicking would not help anything.

"Look," she said. "No one is going to shrink beyond reality. We're closer than we were. At least now we know you have to say some magic words to break the curse. We even have the words." She looked at the parchment in her hand. "We just can't … read them."

"And time, Madam, is running out," hissed Flabberghast, pointing at the clock. "You've stepped into our House, our world. You made me open this envelope and begin the countdown. So *you*, Madam, had better have some answers! Soon! And you –" he pointed at Eric, whose tail drooped considerably – "you are meant to be a housekeeper, are you not? Clean up this blasted mess!"

Then he snatched the parchment out of Nine's hand, turned on his purple-slippered heel and marched into the nearest room. The wooden door slammed shut behind him then instantly melted into nothing, leaving a doorway-shaped, star-speckled blackness in its place.

Nine gasped and cautiously went over to the doorway. Silence and stillness appeared to pour from the hole, if that was even possible. Did she … dare? Slowly, Nine stretched out her left hand and reached for the doorway. Her hand extended towards the nothingness—

Spoon landed on her arm with his spindly legs and rapped her hand with the flat of his blade.

"It means 'Do Not Disturb'," he said firmly,

pointing the sword at her. "Now if you'll excuse me, I've important work to be doing." He sheathed his sword and sprang back upstairs.

Eric lolloped over. "Flabby sad. Flabby think."

"Flab-BER-GHAST!" yelled a muffled voice from the other side of the star-speckled blackness.

Nine looked at the front door and felt a strong desire to be on the other side of it. She looked at the troll, unsure what on earth to do. Eric reached into the front pocket of his frilly apron, pulled out a brown-and-white striped boiled sweet and offered it to Nine. Was this some kind of nasty trick? Eric smiled his wonky, tusky smile.

"Make happy," said Eric, still holding out the sweet.

Nine faltered for a moment, not knowing whether to laugh or cry, thank or scold. And there was a strange, warm feeling in her chest, which was beautiful and terrible at the same time.

"Well," snapped Nine, decisively, "don't."

Nine took the sweet anyway and stared at the gift. The last time someone had given her a gift was the music box – *her* music box. And she'd sworn never to feel so deeply about anything ever again.

She dropped the sweet inside her satchel, refusing to look at the troll. Then, largely for an excuse not to say anything more to the creature, she marched down to the kitchen, righted the table, put the (somehow) still-lidded sugar bowl back on top and flopped down in a chair.

She heard the troll's long toenails scraping along the bricked floor and the sound of the slime-catching bucket being righted. Then she heard him rummaging in the cupboards and, a moment later, he slopped down a silver spoon and a steaming bowl on the table in front of Nine.

"Lady hungry. Lady eat." Nine tried to remember when she had last eaten something hot. Her stomach rumbled. "Food help. Lady think. Make plan." Cautiously, she picked up her spoon and stared at the brown slime. An eyeball bobbed up to the surface and stared back. Nine put the spoon down again.

Flabberghast stomped into the kitchen clutching the witch's letter. He went over to a wooden board hanging on the wall. At the top were painted the words 'TO DO' in golden, sparkly letters. The wizard carefully held the letter so it was nearly – nearly but not quite – touching the board. Suddenly a little fanged mouth sprang out of the wood with a snarl and clasped the parchment firmly and safely in its jaws.

Flabberghast moved his hand away quickly, but not quickly enough.

"Wretched thing!" he grumped, sucking his finger and shaking it in the air. Nine tried to resist a tiny smile as Flabberghast collapsed into the chair opposite her. He said nothing and stared at the table. Eric slopped another bowl in front of him, and put a little napkin beside it.

"Nice soup," he said sadly. He pulled the feather duster from out of his apron. "Eric tidy."

Nine chanced a quick glimpse at the troll. Even his ears were drooping now. He sloped out of the kitchen. Maybe she would brave the soup. She'd eaten plenty of things in the Nest that looked just as bad and probably tasted worse. Picking up her spoon, she dipped it into the bowl as far away from the eyeball as she could manage and brought the soup slowly towards her lips…

There was a sudden loud roar from above them.

"What on earth?!" said Nine, sitting upright in her chair and clattering the spoon back into the bowl.

"Yes, that's correct."

"What?" snapped Nine.

"Nerth. The roaring. It's Wotnerth," said Flabberghast. "A rather undomesticated pet. We picked him up in a swamp just before the curse." He slurped a spoonful of the eyeball soup. "We have no idea what on earth he is. Hence the name. He's just grumpy because it's bath day today. We simply *cannot* wash away the stench of the swamp."

"Why did you pick him up? Why do you pick up anyone … or anything?"

Flabberghast blushed slightly and fiddled with his hat. "Oh, well, it happens like that sometimes. But that was before the curse, when the House moved." Flabberghast gave a little smile. "We had the freedom of the worlds. And the forgotten places between the worlds. Places you could not imagine. Oh, they are truly marvellous."

Nine stared at his eyes. They had changed – they were sparkling with hundreds of silvery flecks, as if tiny shards of diamonds were embedded inside. For that moment something deep and wise and beautifully ancient shone through the boy's eyes – a thousand adventures, a thousand secrets, a thousand years... Then the silvery sparks faded away and the wizard's eyes became blue once more.

"I know I might regret asking this," said Nine, "but how exactly does a toad's tongue move the House?"

"Ah, a most ingenious device on the coat of arms," said the wizard, brightening a little. "You simply pull out the toad's tongue, release and then off the House pops."

"Right," said Nine slowly. She opened her mouth to ask what the toad thought about it all, but Flabberghast's expression darkened.

"She stole the tongue, stole my magic, stole

my freedom." He shifted in his chair and looked away. "Eat up."

Nine looked down at the eyeball in her slime. It blinked.

"I'm not hungry," she said, pushing the bowl away, a teeny, tiny part of her hoping Eric wouldn't notice how full it was.

"You can thank the Dwarvish cookery books for Eric's culinary delights," Flabberghast grumbled. "Still, we should be thankful it's not pancakes. They really shouldn't be furry." He took a mouthful and his eyes widened in alarm. He paused for a moment – then swallowed very hard. Nine could see a spherical lump move down his throat and she couldn't help but smile.

Cookery books.

A spark of inspiration lit up Nine's mind like a candle in a cellar. Her smile grew as a rather good idea clicked into place.

CHAPTER 10

"Your library," said Nine as the wizard wiped the corners of his mouth with the napkin and pushed the half-filled bowl away. "Where the books rearrange themselves. You must have books on spells and curses? About breaking them, maybe? One of them might say how to reveal secret words?"

Flabberghast folded his arms on the table and began banging his head lightly on his arms. "Of course I do, but it's hopeless," he mumbled. "I told you: the library is in a terrible mood since the curse. She made sure we can't find a blasted thing."

Nine walked over and kicked his chair, making him sit up and glare at her. "Take me there."

Flabberghast gave a snort. "Trust me – it's not a good idea, Madam."

"Now," said Nine.

Flabberghast sighed and stood up, muttering about Dwarvish and cookery and knitting sections all the way to the staircase. Nine stared at all the pictures hanging wonkily as they walked up the plum-carpeted stairs. They all featured people who looked decidedly witchy and wizardy: some with pointy hats; some with the same silvery eye-sparkle that Flabberghast had just displayed; all with the same flared nostrils as his.

"*Horatio the Untidy (1508-1649), Millicent the Goat-Eater (1410-1672), Arabella the Belch-Ridden (1702-1836)*," Nine read, studying the titles under each portrait as she went. "Who are you then? Flabberghast the What?"

Flabberghast cleared his throat. "Never mind."

They reached the top of the hallway stairs and Nine took in a sharp breath. The landing was littered with dozens of doors of every size and colour. Some were small as a mousehole, some larger than Eric. There were hundreds of doors and windows dotted all over the ridiculously high walls, which stretched up to an ornate painted ceiling in the distance. There were tall, dark wooden ladders propped up against the walls leading to some of the doors. Other doors looked reachable by a huge spiral staircase that seemed to reach up to the ceiling, or by rickety scaffolds of complicated, wooden staircases that doubled back on themselves with many landings criss-crossing over each other. And then there were doors that didn't appear to be reachable at all.

On one of the landings above them, a plain wooden door opened. A toilet stood in the doorway, then it hopped on its pedestal along the landing. The lid bumped up and down as it moved and a little mischievous giggling came from inside the toilet bowl. Nine and Flabberghast watched as another door opened and the toilet quickly hopped inside. The door slammed shut and there was the loud clanking sound of several bolts and padlocks fastening behind it on the inside, then a muffled, evil giggle. Nine just stared, words failing her yet again.

An extremely narrow staircase on the right led to a single small, thin door. Painted on it was a yellow circle with a smaller circle inside. It wasn't so much the strange symbol on the door as the sickly-smelling smoke wisping from underneath it that drew Nine's attention.

"And that's perfectly normal as well, I suppose?" said Nine, looking at Flabberghast with narrowed eyes.

"It's Dr Spoon's room," said the wizard, thoughtfully. "Apparently, his experiments are going well. If 'going well' means blowing the doors off the hinges twice a week."

Just then, there was a slow, creaking sound above them. Nine turned her head to see a dark purple door at the top of a tall ladder. It opened itself fully, but nothing more happened.

"What now? Why did it do that?" asked Nine.

"That would be *your* room, Madam," replied Flabberghast. "The room chooses the guest, not the other way around. Whatever it is, it's the perfect room for you. When we pick up guests along the way they each have their own perfect space within the House."

"I'm not a guest and I don't want a room."

Flabberghast shrugged. "I presume it's just in case you did. After all, the House at the Edge of Magic has manners." He looked out of the corner of his eye at Nine and added under his breath, "Unlike some."

Nine scowled as Flabberghast led them up a rickety staircase. Each stair creaked and groaned as they touched them. Nine was sure she heard one say "Oof". Up to a short time ago this would have surprised her. Since then, she'd been belched at by a sugar bowl, attacked by a moody streak of light and served eyeball soup by a troll brandishing a feather duster. An oofing staircase was nothing.

They reached a tiny landing at the top. In front of them was a giant green double door with a round brass handle.

"The library, Madam," said Flabberghast. "Now, just so you are aware, the books—"

"I have been to a library before," said Nine. "I'll find my own way around."

"It's not a matter of simply finding the spell section! You do not understand—"

Nine put her hands on her hips. "I *can* read, you know. I understand more than you think!"

"But it's really not a good idea, Madam—"

"We'll see," said Nine, opening one of the doors and stepping inside the room. Quickly, Flabberghast slammed the door behind her.

There was hardly chance to look at the book-lined room in front of her before something rectangular and murderous hurtled towards her at a tremendous pace.

Instinctively Nine ducked, protecting her head with her hands. There was a sharp thud as the thing embedded itself in the door.

Cautiously, she stood up and looked behind her. The 'thing' was a small steel-plated book etched with the title *Wizards' Little Book of Calm*, now sticking out of the wood at an awkward angle. The book jiggled helplessly, trying to wrench itself free. The green double doors were littered with paint-chipped scars. Not the first time this had happened, then.

"You'll have to try harder than that," said Nine to the pathetically jerking book. Then she turned around to face the rest of the library. She looked up. Her eyes widened.

"Er, yes. That's more like it," was all she could manage.

About twenty thick, heavy, leather-bound books hovered in an arc in the air before her, around her and above her. Nine had never thought of books looking in a bad mood, but these definitely did. She inched a little to the right. The books followed her. Then she inched a little to the left. The books still followed her.

Nine looked around. A candelabra hung from the ceiling, candles flickering. The four windowless walls stretched to about three times the height of a normal room and every single space was crammed with bookcases of different shapes and sizes, all piled up and balanced on top of each other, and all crammed with books. Whether or not these would also try to kill her remained to be seen. There were double-sided bookcases mounted on wheels dotted around the room too, and in the middle of the room was a table with a small lectern.

It was bigger and more chaotic than she'd expected. Mr Downes would have had a heart attack at the state of it. Perhaps she should have asked Flabberghast where the spell section was… No. She didn't need him. She would find it herself. She eyed the arc of books above her and took a step forward. The books loomed closer.

"I'm not here for a fight. I'm just here for a book – a book I need to reveal some magic words," said Nine, trying to sound braver than she felt.

She took another step forward. The books loomed closer still. "Fine," said Nine, "have it your way."

She twisted her satchel round so it sat behind her back. Just like a cat: sighting her prey, stalking it quietly, pouncing at the right moment.

Nine's senses were on alert. Her muscles tensed. The books above her swayed, ever so slightly. Nine clenched her fists, stretched her fingers. The thrill of it.

She was on in *three … two … one…*

She dived forward underneath the hovering books, which were clearly not expecting that. They spun around as Nine rolled across the library floor towards the lectern in the middle of the room. The books hurtled after her in a long line – aiming their sharp, heavy corners for her head – when Nine grabbed the lectern and—

BAM! She sent a book flying across the room. It thudded into one of the wheel-mounted bookcases and slid to the floor.

BAM! She sent another one across the room, brushing the candelabra as it went.

Then the books moved out of formation and started randomly swooping at her. Nine swished the lectern in front of her wildly, occasionally getting a strike. She felt an unexpected bang at the back of her head as one struck her.

"OW!" Nine growled, whirling around with the lectern and giving the book a hearty whack.

Two more came at her from different sides. Nine ducked and the first two volumes of *Troll Housekeeping for Beginners* collided and dropped to the floor. A few more whacks with the lectern and the last remaining books dropped lifelessly by her feet. Nine caught her breath. Maybe one of them would be about curse-breaking? She nudged them with her feet, just to check they weren't about to attack again. Nothing.

She glanced at their titles: *101 Recipes for Disaster* … *The Concise Guide to Magic Volume 9* … *How to Cheat at Hopscotch* … *The Art of Disappearing…* Nine stopped. That sounded useful. She reached for it but as her fingertips brushed the book, it completely vanished. Nine tutted. She really hated magic.

She started to move towards one of the wheeled bookshelves. Flabberghast **had** mentioned a spell section, so it must be here somewhere. She just had to find it and—

Then she heard it. A kind of dull rumbly thudding, growing louder and louder. She looked at the wheeled bookcase. The books were shaking. She glanced at the precariously balanced bookcases against the walls. The books there were also vibrating, as if they were stamping on the shelves, striving to break free. The bookcases themselves started wobbling...

Nine swallowed.

Before she had time to think or move, thousands of books shot out of their shelves with such force that all but one of the barely balanced bookcases toppled to the floor, piling on top of each other. But the books pelted down towards Nine and started to form a dark, wobbly wall in front of her – behind her – beside her—

Just above her head the books began to close the gap, overlapping like roof tiles trapping her in a box-like prison. Nine threw herself with all her might against the book-wall nearest the library door – again, again, again – panic rising in her chest. Finally, she burst through, books flying and toppling in every direction.

She ran for the door but books rained down, forging walls on either side, blocking her – this way and that – twisting and turning her path until Nine was running through a book-lined maze with no idea where she was heading. At last she caught a glimpse of green and gold, and sprinted towards it. The door!

Nine leapt for the handle as the books piled up on either side around her. She yanked it open, dislodging the wriggling *Wizards' Little Book of Calm* as she did so. It shot backwards and Nine quickly glanced over her shoulder to see the steel-plated book hurtling towards her once again through an ever-darkening tunnel of books.

She half-ran, half-fell through the doorway, grabbed the handle and slammed it shut. There was the unmistakeable sound of a very uncalm steel-plated book making another dent in the door, followed by the softer thumps of book after book against the wood.

Nine looked up and saw Flabberghast, arms folded, leaning smugly against the bannister at the top of the stairs. She quickly straightened herself up, pulled her satchel back to her hip and resisted the urge to punch his smirking face.

"All done," she said lightly and walked past him with her head held high, deliberately ignoring the sound of the last barely-balanced bookcase crashing to the floor.

CHAPTER 11

Nine marched down the creaking, groaning, oofing staircase as fast as she could for fear that Flabberghast might catch up and interrogate her about the events in the library. She made her way down the various staircases until she found Eric waiting in the entrance hall. He had almost twisted his tail into a knot.

"Lady safe," he said, looking relieved.

"Of course I'm safe."

"Room naughty."

"Yes."

"Books naughty."

"*Yes*," snapped Nine irritably.

"I did tell you it was a bad idea, Madam,"

called Flabberghast smugly from the top of the plum-carpeted stairs.

Nine ignored him and marched to the front door.

"Wait! Wait! Madam! Where are you going?" Flabberghast said, his tone changing from smug to panicked. He began to run down the hallway stairs.

The hands on the clock whizzed backwards, the smallest hand now pointing at the 11. Nine cast a fleeting glance at the tongue-less toad on the coat of arms, then she opened the front door, stepped outside and said, "To a library that doesn't want to kill me."

And, with more than a little satisfaction, she slammed the door behind her.

All the way to the library, Nine's fists were tight, her shoulders up around her ears. Stray cats prowling the streets sprang away to the shadows as she approached. Bonneted ladies walking arm-in-arm stared at her, but Nine didn't care. She cared about breaking the curse. Getting the jewel in that strange, glowing ball. Escaping Pockets' Nest for ever. And not having to return to the House. That House! That horrible, horrible House.

She marched up to the library.

It was so unpredictable!

She pulled open the door and stepped inside.

So unreasonable!

She stormed over to where the librarian was sitting at his desk in the corner, one hand holding his head, the other writing lists of numbers in a large notebook. She slammed her hands down on the desk, rattling the inkwell and making the librarian jump.

"And are *your* books going to try and kill me, Mr Downes?"

"I … don't believe so," the librarian said slowly, straightening his horn-rimmed glasses to look at her more closely.

"Exactly!" said Nine, throwing her hands up in the air before marching off towards the shelves.

She took a deep breath. This was the only place to be when she was really worked up.

Something about the room calmed her down. She ignored the smattering of people. All she saw – all she felt – were the books, their words breathing stories, wisdom, and the only escape and freedom she had ever known.

She closed her eyes, searching for the musty, bookish scent beyond the smell of damp, trying hard to drown out Pockets' voice and the ticking clock in the House. She ran her hands along the line of book spines and was about to lift one at random from the shelf—

"You know you are not permitted to borrow from this library," Mr Downes whispered in her ear.

Nine felt her heart jolt. She whirled around, hands on hips, and looked at the librarian accusingly.

"Another point to me," he said, pulling out his little notebook.

"That doesn't count," Nine burst out.

"Forgive me asking," said Mr Downes as he tucked his notebook back into his jacket, "but are you in trouble? I mean, more than usual."

Nine rubbed her hands over her eyes. *The*

magic words are... "Books on magic," she said in a low voice. "I need books on magic."

The librarian took her by the elbow and pulled her to the side of the room. He glanced around nervously. "I don't know why you would suppose I had books on such things—"

"Mr Downes, I need information," said Nine, looking him in the eye. "Secrets. Magic. Curses." She dropped her voice to a whisper. "Witchcraft."

Mr Downes widened his eyes and shuffled uncomfortably. "I'm really not sure you should be—"

"Do you have anything? *Anything?*"

The librarian sighed and pointed to an ill-lit corner of the room by one of the boarded-up windows.

"Top shelf, in the corner. You'll need the ladder. Don't draw attention to yourself." Nine nodded and went to move but Mr Downes grabbed her elbow. "And I didn't say any of that," he added.

As the librarian rubbed his brow and wandered back to his desk, Nine made her way to the corner. She grasped the bottom of the long, wheeled ladder and pulled it along the shelves towards the darkest corner. She twisted her satchel to her back and up she climbed until she reached the top shelf. She felt a little prickle at the back of her neck … a sense of being somewhere she really shouldn't be. It excited her and terrified her in equal measures. She wanted to look over her shoulder, check she was safe, alone, unwatched, but she didn't dare risk making eye contact with anyone below.

Instead her fingers trailed the soft, dark spines of the books as she read their golden-lettered titles…

Folklore and Legend: A Hunter's Guide…

Hunting what? Nine shook her head. Focus.

An Exploration of Mythical Creatures of Land and Sea…

No, not now.

Spellbinding Methods and Their Efficiency…

Hmm, getting closer.

The Secret Book of Secrets and How to Uncover Them…

YES!

Nine's heart skipped a beat as her fingers lingered over the thick burgundy spine. She reached out to take it from the shelf.

A heavy feeling poured over her, growing stronger and stronger ... like someone was watching. Not from the ground but right there: up on the ladder. Nine shook the irrational feeling from her head, closed her fingers around the spine and pulled the book out—

An eye with a fiercely red iris stared at her from the back of the shelf.

Nine gasped and jolted backwards on the ladder, nearly falling off. The book tumbled from her grasp and, for a split second, she looked away from the eye to watch the book fall towards the ground. It landed with a thud that echoed throughout the room. She looked back at the shelf. The eye was gone.

Heart still pounding, Nine scrambled down the ladder as fast as she could. She snatched the book from the wooden floor and quickly headed for the exit. Mr Downes was at his desk, leaning over his book of figures, worry lines creased all over his usually genial face. He looked up as Nine walked past. "I trust you found what you were looking for?"

"More than I was looking for!" said Nine over her shoulder. She tucked the book into her satchel and walked out into the street. As she weaved her way through the back alleys towards the House, the roads grew narrower, the people fewer. Nine's thoughts turned to the red eye in the library. It had been watching her. Definitely watching her. Perhaps a warning—

"THIEF!" bellowed a voice behind her.

Nine jumped out of her thoughts, legs twitching, ready to run. She whirled around to see the ruddy-cheeked butcher from the market speeding towards her, his blood-splattered apron flapping.

"Does anyone *not* want to kill me today?" she snapped, before she turned and ran.

"I'll teach you a lesson!" bellowed the butcher.

"Only if you catch me!" Nine said as she sprinted along the dirty, uneven ground. There was a small passageway on the right. She dashed down it. That would show the—

A sickening feeling hit the bottom of her stomach like a stone and she came to a halt. No. Oh no.

This was a dead end.

Nine whirled around. The puffing butcher appeared at the end of the passage, striding towards her. Nine felt panic rising in her chest. She looked around. Walls. She slammed her hands against the rough bricks. Just walls everywhere. The butcher advanced. Nine's breathing grew faster.

Think. *Think*.

"Oh yes, I've caught you, thief," the butcher said, stretching out his arm.

THINK!

Suddenly there was a blur of red, and Nine had the unpleasant feeling of being sucked through solid fog. It seemed to squeeze her chest and, for a moment, she stopped breathing. Everything grew dark and silent until, with a strange popping feeling, she felt herself stagger backwards – able to see, able to breathe.

Nine regained her balance. She heard the muffled yell of surprise from the butcher and heard heavy footsteps running away. She was now inside the building, on the other side of the wall...

And she wasn't alone.

CHAPTER 12

Four large flickering candles stood on the floor, one in each corner of the empty room. Empty, except for the figure – a young woman – standing an arm's length away. She had her back towards Nine, a long, silky tumble of red hair and wore an elaborate, shapely, black crinoline dress.

Nine studied the figure. No sound. No movement. What should she do? There didn't even seem to be a door out of this room. Maybe she was meant to approach her. Maybe the woman was here to help…

The figure made a sharp twisting motion with her wrist. Nine's satchel was snatched away by an invisible hand. She stared as it spiralled up into the air, sending the book flying out. There was an unexpectedly deafening thud as it landed on the floor beside Nine, followed by a softer thud as the satchel dropped on top of it.

Maybe she *wasn't* here to help…

"A little bedtime reading?" said the figure.

"Who are you?" Nine demanded. Her hands instinctively formed into fists, although she suspected that in any kind of fight with this person, a skinny thiefling would not be coming out on top. "Did you just pull me through a wall?"

Nine took a step forward.

"Well, well, look at *you*," said the woman. "I knew they were desperate, but dear, dear."

"What? Who?" said Nine, her muscles tensing. "There's nothing wrong with me."

"No?" The woman barely stifled a giggle. Nine couldn't see her face but she could hear the bubble of laughter in the woman's voice. "If there truly *is* nothing wrong with you, nothing wrong with your life, then why knock on the tiny door?"

Nine said nothing.

"Oh, there will be consequences," the young woman continued slowly, in a sing-song voice. A smooth voice. A dangerous voice. A voice that oozed like deadly lava. Nine froze.

"If you get involved. And you *are* involved, aren't you? Shame. There's still time to change your mind – it's not too late. Go back to your pitiful little life. Because there's nothing wrong with you … is there? Your life is *perfectly fine*."

"Who are you?" Nine repeated, trying to steady her voice.

"A friend," said the woman with a tinkly laugh that sounded about as friendly as a poisoned knife in the ribs, "bringing you a friendly warning. Do not get involved."

Nine edged closer. "Turn around then, friend. Show me your face," said Nine, pushing her feet deeper into the ground. She was ready for whatever was coming next. "Show me!"

Silence.

In a sudden rush of frustration, Nine marched in front of the woman – but with a strange, unnatural speed, the woman turned around so

Nine saw just her back again. Nine hesitated for a moment, took a deep, quiet breath, then walked around to the other side. But again the figure turned. Just the back of her long, red hair.

Again Nine ran around the black-clad figure, but the young woman just spun faster and faster, her hair a scarlet blur. Nine stopped suddenly. So did the woman: with her back towards Nine. She laughed a laugh that would freeze rivers.

"Is that really the best you can do? Dear, dear. I suppose they *will* shrink beyond reality then. It'll be terribly fun to watch. Terribly."

"Stop it!" cried Nine, her chest heaving.

"Don't say I didn't warn you. Foolish girl."

Rage, fear, confusion – everything bubbled up inside Nine and she lunged out at the strange woman, grabbing her arm. But as she did so, the figure disintegrated into a small heap of red dust. Nine gasped and quickly snatched back her hand, her heart thumping. "Consequences," came a bodiless whisper as the red dust trickled away through a gap in the floorboards.

Still staring at the spot where the woman

had stood, Nine backed away slowly towards her satchel and hurriedly stuffed the book back inside.

"Whoever you are," she said to the last red specks, as they disappeared between the floorboards, "I think 'friend' might be a bit hopeful."

A slightly sick feeling settled in her chest. What was she doing? She was tangled up in this strange magic, out of her depth … but wasn't anything – *anything* – better than spending the rest of her life in the Nest?

"I'm not afraid," Nine lied to the room, marching over to the wall she had entered through.

The four candles in the corners suddenly extinguished themselves, plunging Nine into pitch blackness. A little chill ran down Nine's spine. She quickly thrust her hand into the not-really bricks. There was the irresistible force of being sucked through solid fog once more…

Darkness … silence … chest squeeze and then…

POP. The walls spat her out and she tumbled to the ground. She picked herself up and dusted herself down.

"I hate magic," Nine said, and headed for the House.

CHAPTER 13

When Eric opened the door, his look of delight was quickly replaced by one of concern.

"Lady pale," he said.

"Lady fine," snapped Nine, and pushed her way in. She noticed the smallest sword hand on the hexagonal clock was pointing at the 8. "Lady always fine."

As she passed him the troll quickly rummaged in his apron pocket, presumably trying to find a sweet, but Nine marched on. Flabberghast staggered down the stairs, wearing most of a suit of armour. One of the arms had been half pulled off, his helmet was askew and there were several large dents in the breastplate. More curiously, he

117

was also splattered with bubbles and looked on the soggy side of wet. He removed his helmet and soapy water poured out.

Nine rolled her eyes. "Why?" she asked in a bored tone.

"Bath. Wotnerth," panted Flabberghast, placing the helmet on the plum carpet. "Thank the stars that's over for another week." His face turned grim. "If we survive another week."

Nine held up *The Secret Book of Secrets and How to Uncover Them* and Flabberghast's expression turned from half-drowned misery to delight. He clapped his hands together, sending a billow of bubbles floating up into the air.

"An excellent find!" he said, taking the book. He tried to open it but the cover refused to budge. He let out a sigh. "Ah. Small print."

"What?" said Nine.

Flabberghast pointed at tiny, silvery words written at the bottom of the front cover then read aloud, "*To open, whisper a secret to me.*" He frowned, then brought the book up to his mouth and whispered something. His face turned slightly red. Nine strained her ears but couldn't hear.

The cover sprang open, bopping Flabberghast on the nose. "Madam, this does indeed look most useful."

"It had better be," said Nine. "Because I am *not* getting another one. Which reminds me." She walked briskly into the kitchen followed by the book-bearing wizard and the troll, marched over to the tea cupboard and grabbed the handle.

ZAP. She ignored the fact she now had flippers for feet and turned around to glare at the others. Flabberghast had a pumpkin head with three eyes blinking in the middle. The book exploded into worms, which wriggled away. A gush of green liquid appeared from nowhere just above Flabberghast's head and drenched him. Nine turned to look at Eric, who had grown another four pairs of arms and sprouted a long, curved beak.

She narrowed her eyes. "That," said Nine, "was for not warning me about your *friend*." She put feathery hands on her hips, hoping they were taking her seriously even though she had a chicken perched on her head. And perhaps they were, until the chicken laid an egg. The magic began to fade.

"I beg your pardon, Madam?" said Flabberghast. "What friend?"

"The kind that isn't very friendly! You could have told me she's dangerous!" Nine gestured wildly with her hands. "I thought she was off in some magical land but she's out there – on the streets! I got squeezed through a wall! Twice!"

Flabberghast swallowed. "The witch. She's onto us. What did she say?"

Nine paused, feeling strangely reluctant to pass on the warning. That Nine wasn't up to the job. That she should walk away while she could. That if she was involved, there would be consequences...

"Nothing, really ... just crowing over the fact you're going to be shrunk beyond reality."

Flabberghast swallowed again. "I propose, Madam, that we examine this book without delay." Flabberghast put it down on the kitchen table and sat awkwardly into a chair, his armour clanking.

Nine and Eric took their seats. The sugar bowl belched at Nine, who irritably clamped her hand over its lid. There was the strange, spluttering sound of something uncomfortably swallowing its own smoke, then the sugar bowl was still.

Flabberghast turned to the contents page of the book and ran his unarmoured finger down the list. "*Secret-Keeping for Beginners … How to Conceal a Dragon in Your Bedroom…*" he muttered as Nine peered over his shoulder.

A muffled, stony grinding noise came from the arched door in the corner of the kitchen.

"Another part of the House I should know about?" said Nine, looking suspiciously towards the door.

"Just the cellar," muttered Flabberghast, still running his fingers down the contents list.

"Well, what's that strange noise coming from it?"

The wizard flapped a hand at her. "Madam! Enough! I'm trying to concentrate. It's just the Sometimes Dead – perfectly normal."

Nine sighed, really not feeling the words

"Sometimes Dead" and "perfectly normal" deserved to be so close together. If something was only dead *sometimes*, what on earth was it the rest of the time?

"*Enter Secret Places: How to Make a Skeleton Key...* Aha!" The wizard slammed his finger onto the book halfway down the page. "*Revelato Potion: How to Reveal Invisible Words*! That'll show us the magic words on the letter! Here we go. 'The Revelato Potion burns through the protective magic which conceals letters and writings.' Marvellous!" Flabberghast trailed his finger along the page.

"'Collecting deadly nightshade by moonlight'... yes, yes, yes ... 'mix with water'... Aha! 'Revealing words which are intended to be secret is a serious matter and should only be undertaken in the gravest and direst of circumstances.' Well, this is grave and dire. We are to be shrunk into oblivion – *and* there's no tea!

"'To ensure it is not undertaken lightly, the revealed words can only be read, spoken, discussed or understood by those individuals willing to...' Oh. Oh, very interesting ... 'each person needing to participate must willingly'... Hmm. Yes, of course. Makes perfect sense." He cleared his throat and tapped the book decisively with his finger.

"What?" Nine said sharply.

"Hm" asked Flabberghast, looking up with unconvincing wide eyes and an even more unconvincing wide smile.

"Each person needing to participate must willingly WHAT?"

"Oh. That. Yes." The wizard shuffled and examined his chewed fingernails. "Must simply add an item of great personal and emotional significance to be sacrificed."

"Eric give?"

"All of you, actually," said Flabberghast, shuffling his feet. He walked over to the TO DO board, his remaining armour clunking as he went. The little motionless jaws were still clamped around the letter. "'You will need all the help you can get from your ridiculous companions'," he read, narrowing his eyes in annoyance.

Eric's face fell. "Eric things?"

"Needs must," Flabberghast said briskly and took a deep breath. He clunked back over to Eric, stood as tall as he could, looked the troll in the eye … and snatched the feather duster.

Eric let out a roar and snatched it back. But Flabberghast was prepared and grabbed the other end until the feather duster went back-and-forth in the most bizarre game of tug-of-war that Nine had ever seen. She watched the hopeless situation for a moment until Flabberghast crashed into the table, making the sugar bowl puff out a huge, green cloud of smoke.

"OI! STOP!" she yelled, waving her hand to clear the green smoke. She yanked on Eric's side of the feather duster, sending both herself and Eric tumbling backwards and Flabberghast crashing forwards onto the floor.

Eric let out a high-pitched whimper and, with the unnatural speed of a troll about to be deprived of his precious feather duster, he darted up the staircase. Nine and Flabberghast looked at each other, scrambled to their feet and ran up the stairs, two at a time, after him – Flabberghast clunking as he went.

They found Eric up a couple of flights of criss-crossing staircases, on a landing with a closet. It was made of plain, dark wood and looked shoddily made and strangely out of place. The troll wrung his tail and Nine ignored the feeling of pity she couldn't possibly have felt for the creature. Tough. It had to be done.

"Eric," she said as they slowly advanced towards him. "Where's the duster?"

"No duster." Eric shook his head.

"Come on! Where is it?" said Flabberghast. "We cannot get the magic words and break the curse without a personal sacrifice."

"Duster gone." The troll pulled an odd expression, making his lopsided face even more lopsided. Nine could only guess he was attempting to look clever, which really didn't suit him.

Nine sighed and walked over to the closet. She yanked open the door. Her eyebrows raised only the tiniest fraction.

"There's a skeleton in the closet," she said to Flabberghast.

The wizard froze, then broke into an enormously fake, nervous-looking smile. He flapped an arm at her. "Shhh! We don't mention that!"

Nine stared for a second at the tall, presumably human, skeleton in the wardrobe, its bones all somehow held together in place – including the hand now holding a feather duster. She narrowed her eyes suspiciously.

"Just as odd as the rest of them," she muttered, plucking the duster from its grasp and shutting the door in its unsettling, bony face.

"How rude," came a deep voice from the wardrobe.

Nine paused, but only for a second. There was only so much surprise a person could feel in one day, and Nine was beginning to feel she'd already had her fair share. "Did that skeleton just speak?"

Flabberghast took the duster from her hand. "Not now, Madam. We have more pressing things to attend to."

"Eric duster!" Eric wailed, his eyes filling with

tears. He pulled his tail up towards his face and wiped his eyes with the fluffy end.

Nine refused to look at him but could see him slump to the floor out of the corner of her eye. "It's just a duster," she said harshly.

"Just duster!" howled Eric, beating the floor with his fist.

Spoon's little door flung open on the staircase to the right. An odd smell like toasted dung wafted out as the kilted spoon marched towards them.

"What in the devil's name is going on?" he growled. "Calm that beast down, lad. I'm trying to concentrate! If I can nae get this timing right, I warn you, there'll be an almighty—"

PHWOOSH! A fountain of purple liquid erupted somewhere behind the spoon. A splat landed on his head. The spoon closed his eyes in frustration, tightened his mouth and drew his little hands into fists.

Flabberghast twisted around on his armoured heels and fixed the spoon with a huge smile. He threw wide his arms.

"Ah, Dr Spoon!" he said, clasping his hands

together. "Good news! As it transpires, *all* we need to do to acquire the magic curse-breaking words is *merely* collect a plant, add an item of great personal sacrifice, and then this *small* misunderstanding will be—"

"Sacrifice?" said Spoon, looking like he was about to explode ... if wooden spoons could explode. Nine would not be at all surprised. He slid down the banister and flew off the end at great speed. He curled himself into an awkward ball of wood and tartan, landing impressively on the floor and rolling to a stop at Flabberghast's feet. Eric stopped wailing.

The spoon put his spindly arms on his not-actually-there hips. "You know, lad, I'm beginning to regret stepping inside this House."

"Yet, as I recall, *you* were the one desperately hitching a lift!" retorted Flabberghast.

"Aye, and so would you, laddie, if you had the devil on your tail!" grumbled the spoon. "You promised me you'd help me find Professor Dish—"

Nine's ears pricked up. "Wait ... who?"

"Professor Dish," said the spoon, still glaring at Flabberghast. "We were separated after an experiment … went wrong. She is my partner."

"In crime?" asked Nine automatically.

"In alchemy."

"Alchemy? Turning things to gold?" asked Nine, glancing up at Dr Spoon's room, longing to see what was inside. A large blob of purple goo dropped from the doorframe onto the staircase. "That doesn't look like gold."

"I must find that dish. I have one half of the answer. She has the other. This moron –" he gestured to the wizard – "picks me up, promises me we'll find her, then gets us all cursed and trapped in the House! Three years it's been!"

Flabberghast cleared his throat. "Ah, which makes it so marvellous, does it not, that the breaking of the curse is at last within our reach! Just that tiny matter of a sacrifice."

"Aye. I'll do it – for the professor," said the spoon. "Take it – the thing I hold most dear, my family heirloom. Proudly worn. And proudly sacrificed." There was a blur of spindly fingers and then his kilt dropped to the floor, leaving him standing there, hands on hips, in a pair of orange, flowery pants.

"Oh! Goodness!" muttered Flabberghast, covering his eyes with his hands. "Do – do go and put something... I hope – I *do* hope – you must have more clothes?"

Nine snorted as the spoon hurled the tiny kilt at the wizard, who caught it with fumbling hands.

"Aye," said Spoon. "Now let's get this curse broken." He hopped back up the staircase to the tiny door and slammed it shut.

Nine folded her arms. "Come on then. Eric's duster, Spoon's kilt. What are *you* going to put in?"

Flabberghast looked up at her sharply. "Me? Oh... Yes, Madam. I have just the thing." He straightened his breastplate, grabbed the duster and the kilt, and clunked his way down to the hallway. Nine looked at Eric sitting with his large, trunk-like knees tucked up to his chin. Should she say something? But what? What *did* you say to a troll who had just lost his feather duster?

She wasn't sure anyone in the whole world could answer that one.

There came a despairing wizard kind of roar from downstairs. "Oh, what now?" said Nine and ran down as fast as she could, closely followed by the troll.

They came to a halt in the hallway where Flabberghast was clutching the duster and the kilt in one hand, and pointing at the empty, glassless display cabinet with the other.

"My hopscotch trophy!" bellowed Flabberghast. "Where is my hopscotch trophy? When I said 'tidy up', I expected it to be put back!" Eric started twisting his tail and his eyes darted to the cupboard under the stairs. There was the sign, written on parchment in black ink and tacked onto the door with an iron pin: NEVER OPEN THIS DOOR.

Flabberghast turned as white as the moon. "You didn't?" he said in a very low voice.

"Mmm," Eric said in a very high voice.

"Tell me you didn't."

"Mmm."

131

Nine felt her patience rapidly reaching boiling point. "WHAT?"

"You didn't put it in the cupboard under the stairs."

"Eric quick. Eric open. Eric throw. Eric shut."

"WHY DID YOU PUT IT IN THE—"

Nine's patience passed boiling point. "Then for goodness sake just get it back! Whatever is in there can't be that bad!" She marched over to the cupboard under the stairs.

"No!" yelled Flabberghast. "Never—"

Then Nine yanked the door open. And screamed.

CHAPTER 14

What happened next was so quick that Nine barely had time to register it. There was a deafening clatter, a rush of colour – and a chaos of clutter poured out like an avalanche. A brass hooter, a troll-sized raincoat, a large collection of glowing hammers, a 'Complete Family Set of Pop-Up Coffins', strange-looking scientific instruments, cauldrons of various sizes, a picnic blanket, a 'Vampire Starter Kit', a massive leather-bound book, numerous pieces of parchment, an InkFree quill in a box, an oversized green woollen dragon…

Nine sat buried neck-high in the heap, catching her breath. Something on her left that looked like a blue ball of wool on legs scurried away. She stared at the pile that surrounded her, then she stared at Flabberghast and Eric.

"Years of tidying! That sign was there for a reason!" raged Flabberghast, waving his arms so wildly that the remaining arm of his armour fell off. "And now we'll never find the trophy!"

"At least I tried!" Nine attempted to wriggle under all the clutter. A troll-sized pair of pants fell on her head. "Come on! DO something!"

Eric reached forward, scrabbling at piles of stuff until Nine's shoulders were clear. Then he grabbed her with one hand, half-shaking, half-pulling her free. Nine wrestled herself from his grasp as soon as she could.

"I'm fine!" she snapped, clambering awkwardly over the mountain of mess. "Right, let's find that trophy."

"No, come back!" said Flabberghast.

But Nine was already inside the dark cupboard, scrabbling around. "Come on!"

"You mustn't go in—"

"Stop making excuses and find that trophy! I need that 'immeasurable wealth' you—"

Nine stopped. There was a strange, juddering sound. The mountain of mess shifted beneath her, making her lose her balance. She fell back onto her bottom. Silence. Then another strange, juddering sound. The mess moved again.

"Flabberghast," Nine said slowly, "what is going on?"

The wizard sighed. "The only way we could fit it all into the cupboard was to put a compacting spell on it years ago. The cupboard squashes everything up."

"Everything?" squeaked Nine. Suddenly, there was a grinding sound as the walls of the cupboard began moving closer. Nine felt herself being lifted higher as the mess was pushed upwards. She tumbled left and right, trying and failing to keep her balance. As everything around was squished and squashed and shoved higher and higher, a flash of silver caught Nine's eye.

"I can see it!" Nine gasped. She threw herself towards the trophy but it disappeared under a chamber pot decorated with stars. Nine fell backwards. There was a strange, sucking feeling as the mess in the hallway was drawn back into the cupboard. Large, glowing hammers flew around her. A small metal tripod hurtled towards her; Nine felt the sharp sting as it grazed her cheek.

"Come out!" yelled Flabberghast.

"I can get it!" Nine rummaged under a skull-embroidered cushion. Her hands touched cool, smooth silver – then she was tipped backwards, upwards, and her hair brushed the top of the ceiling. She rolled sideways but was pushed back against the wall. She lunged forwards again, reached out, grabbed it—

"MADAM!"

The cauldron bumped into her. Nine could feel herself being pulled back, squashed up. She was going to end her days buried, suffocated, crushed, in a mountain of junk. She felt everything close in around her and now she could hardly breathe—

She grasped the trophy in her hands and threw herself sideways towards the doorway. She felt huge, rough hands grabbing her, her satchel being tugged, as with a deafening sucking noise the remaining stuff hurtled past her into the cupboard.

The door slammed shut behind her. The sign fell off with a quiet tap. Silence.

Nine caught her breath. She became aware that she was in a tangled heap of wizard, troll, feather duster and girl, and shook herself free. She glanced at the cupboard door, then at Eric's deep yellow eyes and wished, somehow, that she felt able to say two simple words to the troll.

But "thank you" wasn't part of her vocabulary. It meant you owed someone something. And Nine didn't ever want that ever again. She was on her own against this world and that was how she liked it – because the world had turned its back on her. It never brought you strawberries.

All she could say, as they staggered to their feet, was, "I said I was fine!"

"And the sign said 'Never open this door'," said Flabberghast curtly.

"Well, I was never very good at doing what I was told."

"Clearly!"

Nine looked down at the hopscotch trophy

in her hand and slammed it into Flabberghast's breastplate.

"You're welcome," she said.

"Lady hurt," said Eric, his mouth all downturned. He frantically began rummaging in his apron.

Nine became aware of the stinging and put a hand up to her cheekbone. She saw the smear of blood on her fingers.

"Just a scratch." She glared at the trophy scornfully, reading the inscription carved along the base. "'FLABBERGHAST. WORLD HOPSCOTCH CHAMPION 1835.' Your most precious possession? I can't believe it's for *hopscotch*."

"Clearly, Madam, you have no appreciation of the challenge of wizard hopscotch."

"Which, by the way," snapped Nine, "I'm completely fine with." She brushed her cheek again but refused to acknowledge the blood or the pain. Pain was weakness. Never show weakness.

She looked at the hexagonal clock, the three larger sword-shaped hands still whizzing backwards, and the smallest hand now pointing at the 7. "What now?"

Flabberghast looked at Nine. "The book specified that all persons who need to be involved must donate an item of personal sacrifice."

"Yes, you've done that," said Nine.

Flabberghast tilted his head slightly. "All persons. That, Madam, includes you."

"What?" said Nine, throwing her hands in the air. "I've got nothing to do with it!"

"Ah, but you have," said Flabberghast, waggling a finger at her. "I believe, as curse-breaker, your fate is now bound up with ours. You are, one might say, *involved*."

Nine felt a little chill down her spine as she remembered the lava-voiced words of the faceless witch. *And you are involved, aren't you?*

"I'm not … involved," Nine said, more to the voice in her head than to Flabberghast.

"I beg to differ, Madam."

"Beg away!" retorted Nine as a growing sense of unease crept over her. The House shrinking into nothing, vanishing for ever… It hadn't occurred to her that she might disappear inside it too. And an item of personal sacrifice? There was only one thing it could be…

"You must bring your item, Madam, then the book specifies to place them in the cauldron, sprinkle them with water mixed with deadly nightshade gathered by moonlight." Flabberghast looked towards the kitchen. "There's some in the back garden. Then, one can only hope, the magic words will be revealed. We speak them – and the curse is broken."

"And I get the floaty red ball with the jewel that's worth a lot?"

"You receive the levitating scarlet orb which holds a jewel of immeasurable wealth, Madam."

And freedom, Nine thought.

"Fine," she said. "I'll come back tonight. And this had better work."

CHAPTER 15

As she wound her way through the streets towards Pockets' Nest, Nine wondered how many people in the history of history had nearly gotten crushed in a cupboard full of magical junk. The sooner she could say goodbye to that House – the sooner she could get on with the rest of her life – the better. She passed the library and watched as Mr Downes locked the door. He stared sadly up at the near-derelict building. As he turned he noticed Nine, tipped his hat and gave a weary smile before he strolled away down the street.

Slowly, heavily, Nine walked on to Whinney's Passage, turned down the alleyway and knocked on the terrace door. "No strawberries today," she whispered.

Then she froze. Her heavy, tired senses burst into wakefulness. Someone was behind her. She could sense them staring at her back. Her breathing became quicker. She curled her hands into fists, widened her eyes, whirled round—

Nothing. No one. She looked left and right.

Wait… What was that, farther up the alley? Nine squinted. Something like a tiny little red light in the air? She tried to focus…

Then an arm shot out of the warehouse, roughly pulled her inside and slammed the door. Nine tumbled down through the trapdoor and into the Nest. Every now and then she managed to land on her feet – thanks to years of practice – and today was one of those days. When she looked up, she found Pockets glaring up at her from his bed. Nine felt a sickening lurch as she saw him holding the little music box – *her* music box – in his hands.

"Where has you been, girl?" slurred Pockets.

"Out," she said warily, waiting for the inevitable next question.

"What you bring for Nockets' Pest?"

"Er…"

"Worst thiefling in the world!" wailed Pockets, sitting up and pointing a wavering finger at Nine. "Useless! You's all useless!" He waved his hand at the cellar. Mary and the others wisely slunk back into the shadows. "Go live on the streets then! See if Pockets cares! No freedom, no life, *nothing*." The old man slumped down onto his bed and the melancholy tinkling of the music box filled the cellar. Nine's heart stung at the sound. "Pockets took you in. Never strawberries," Pockets slurred and sniffed loudly. "Never."

The music box tinkled on. Nine crept to her corner, waiting twitchily. She brushed her fingers over the library book on her bed but this was no time for reading. After what seemed like for ever, the sound of the tinkling music was replaced with the sound of loud, even snoring. Nine stood up and tiptoed towards the old man. Her heart sank as she saw he still clutched the little music box in his grimy hand, his fingers curled around it.

Just like a cat: sighting her prey, stalking it quietly, pouncing at the right moment.

Pockets stirred. Nine froze.

"Never…" he murmured.

Nine held her breath.

"Strawberries…"

Life had never brought him anything, either. A pang of pity stung Nine's heart and she fought it down. The old man let out a loud, rattling snore.

Nine breathed again. Her senses were on alert. Her muscles tensed. One wrong move and the moment was gone. She moved into position, clenched her fists, stretched her fingers – her pre-pounce ritual.

She was on in *three*…

She swallowed down the tight, choking feeling in her throat.

Two…

Focus on the prey.

One…

This was everything.

Go!

Her heart thumped in her ears as she reached for the silver box. She started sliding it out from the old man's fingers, not daring to breathe. Her fingertip knocked the tiny handle and – her heart leapt – tinkling notes rang out.

Pockets snorted and stirred, his grip tightened – this time around Nine's fingers. For one sad, strange moment, Nine held her music box and Pockets held Nine's hand. Then the moment vanished into memory. Pockets' grip slackened and he began to snore again, his rotten breath wafting over Nine. She slipped the music box free, dropped it into her satchel and softly stepped backwards … and backwards … and backwards…

There was a sudden rustling behind her.

"Hey!" Tom stood there half-awake but pointing at Nine. "Pockets! She's—"

Nine leapt forward and clasped her hand over his mouth. "No!" she hissed, looking him in the eyes. Tom glared back and tried to pull her hand away.

"Please," she whispered urgently. "This was mine, always mine, and now I have to take it back. I have to get away. Please keep quiet and I'll let you have something."

Tom's expression softened and his body relaxed. Nine unclasped her hand from his mouth.

"There's a book on my bed," Nine whispered, glancing over her shoulder as Pockets stirred again. "Go and get it, look at all the squiggly letters. Someone I know can teach you to read them. It's incredible. Just take it to the library when you're ready. All right? And sniff those pages – they smell really good."

Tom nodded uncertainly. Nine nodded back as the boy began tiptoeing over towards Nine's bed.

"And Tom?" The boy looked up, his face half-covered in shadow. Nine gave a little smile. "Let the librarian catch you."

The boy looked thoughtful as he slipped away to claim his prize.

Pockets snored on, unaware of the best thiefling in the world. Nine tiptoed across the cellar towards the dangling rope in the corner. Time to get that deadly nightshade, break the curse and get her own strawberries.

She put both hands on the rope, ready to climb. She paused for a moment and, with one last look at the place she called home, Nine clambered up the rope and flew the Nest.

CHAPTER 16

As she scurried through the dark, chilly streets, Nine glanced up at the sky. The ghostly orb of the moon was barely visible behind a huge, thick cloud; not the most hopeful start when you had to pick a plant by moonlight. She sighed and marched on, clutching her precious treasure, aware that everything now rested on a curse, a glowing red ball and the promise of a hopscotch-obsessed wizard.

Snatches of melancholy music tinkled as the music box jolted around inside the satchel. But now, as she neared the House, Nine could not bear to hear it. She knocked on the doorknocker, forcing back the burning, prickling feeling that threatened to overrun her eyes. The troll, wearing a fluffy yellow dressing gown, opened the door and stared at her.

"MOVE!" she barked, the troll already stepping aside. And if she felt the sweet pushed into her hand as she passed by, she made absolutely sure she didn't let on.

"Make haste, Madam!" cried Flabberghast as Nine entered the kitchen. "The moon may shine at any moment!" He was still in his indigo pyjamas and purple slippers, topped now with a well-worn blue nightcap.

The spoon swung into view wearing – to everyone's great relief – tartan pyjamas. He landed at Nine's feet. "About time," he muttered.

Flabberghast glanced nervously at the cauldron beside him. "You have brought your item of personal sacrifice?"

Nine said nothing but reached inside her satchel. Her hand closed around the little music box and didn't move.

"Madam! Did you bring it?"

"Yes!" said Nine as she walked across the

kitchen. Slowly she pulled it out of the satchel and held it above the cauldron. She looked at the sacrificed items: the feather duster, the kilt, the trophy...

"Madam, make haste! Unless you wish us all to be shrunk beyond reality –"

"No shrink! Eric shrink!"

"– I must urge you to––"

"YES!" snapped Nine. "FINE!" She tilted her hand slowly ... slowly ... until the music box – her beloved music box – finally dropped from her palm into the cauldron. It landed with a soft thud on the feather duster, tinkling one last note, and then it was silent. She closed her eyes for a heartbeat, feeling a strange lump in her throat. Swallowing it down, she whirled around to the wizard.

"This," she hissed, narrowing her eyes, "had better be worth it."

"Yes, yes, yes, yes, yes," Flabberghast muttered irritably as he pushed Nine to the back door. "Now listen, this is deadly nightshade." He held up *The Secret Book of Secrets and How to Uncover*

Them and pointed at the picture of a plant with little purple flowers. "I distinctly remember there was some down by the angel statue."

"Angel statue?"

"You can't miss it. Two wings, curly hair, looks rather grumpy. The moment that moon shines on the garden, Madam, pick the nightshade!"

Nine turned around to look at them. "But you're coming too?"

Flabberghast cleared his throat and Eric moved beside him, tail in hand. "Ah, now, regrettably, we cannot step foot into the back garden either, Madam. The witch made sure of that."

Nine frowned.

"You're on your own, lass," said Spoon. "But we're right behind you."

Flabberghast opened the back door. "More or less," he said – and shoved Nine outside.

A light breeze had picked up, bringing the scent of damp moss. Nine looked up at the sky. The moon was still behind the blanket of cloud. But with the wind blowing gently that could change at any moment … she hoped.

Without a host of furious, spear-wielding goblins crowding around the back door, Nine could make out some shadowy shapes. Tall ... thin ... sloping ... dotted all over the ground like...

"Graves," said Nine. "Your back garden is a *graveyard*?" She turned around to see the others huddled together in the doorway watching her.

"We never really bothered with landscaping," Flabberghast said with a finality that implied that this was all the explanation Nine was going to get.

"So I see." She took a few steps forward and stared at the shadowy, forlorn stones.

"Be ready for the moonlight, Madam," said Flabberghast. "Don't stay in the garden a moment longer than you must. Return to us as quickly as you possibly can. Which reminds me –" Flabberghast pointed up at the sky – "it's still Wednesday for the moment, so watch out for the—"

There was a sudden flittering noise behind Nine. She whirled around to see a cloud-like mass of black moving at great speed across the sky towards them. Nine stared at it, her heart missing a beat. Suddenly a giant black creature, as big as an open umbrella, swooped down towards her out of nowhere. Instinctively Nine crouched down, raised her satchel over her head and lashed out.

There was a thud. Nine's heart thumped as she opened her eyes to see a giant bat spinning wildly through the air and landing behind a pyramid-shaped tomb.

"Bad bat," whimpered Eric from the back door.

"Madam, take cover!" bellowed Flabberghast.

Nine shook her head. "No! I'm finding the nightshade. I can handle bats."

"Yes but we didn't mention their serious digestive problems, did we, Madam?"

"WHAT?"

Droppings the size of a saucer started to splat on the grassy ground right in front of her feet. Nine leapt backwards. There was a fizzing, sizzling noise and spirals of smoke came up from the ground. When it cleared, Nine gasped as she saw that the area all around was burnt.

"Do *not* let their droppings touch you!" hissed Flabberghast.

"I'll try and remember that," called Nine as she ran behind a gravestone, which leaned at an unnerving, unhelpful angle.

Another giant bat dived towards her. Nine scrabbled around on the ground and found a small loose stone. She hurled it at the bat and ducked down again behind the gravestone. The creature circled for a moment then aimed its bottom towards her. The slop hit the gravestone with a splat, followed by a sizzle.

Nine twisted her satchel behind her back and ran wildly across the graveyard as the bats followed, shooting droppings all around her.

"Find that nightshade, lass! Left a bit!" yelled Spoon.

"No, it's right a bit!" called Flabberghast. "Er … isn't it?"

"Garden dark!" wailed Eric. "Where lady?"

"Don't you know where it is?!" Nine yelled back at them, ducking behind another tall gravestone.

There was another sizzling splat, which oozed down the side of the stone.

"Madam, kindly remember it's been years since I've stepped outside," came Flabberghast's indignant voice. "I cannot be expected to remember the precise location of every single—"

"FINE!" yelled back Nine, putting her hands over her head as another bat flew overhead. "I'll find it myself!" And, taking a deep breath, she darted out from behind the grave – and ran.

"Madam? Madam?" came Flabberghast's now-distant voice. "Where are you?"

Nine ignored him. She looked wildly at the sloping stones of various shapes and sizes. *Where? Where was the angel?* She ran over tufted mounds of grass and moss, pausing and crouching among the gravestones. The garden seemed to go on for ever.

Focus. *Focus.*

There! She could see the shadowy shape of a pair of wings. She wove through the graves past a tall, pointy monument overgrown with greenery – and there it was. An angel: two wings, curly hair and looking like it had swallowed a rotten lemon.

"Found the angel!" Nine yelled, dropping to the ground and frantically searching for the plant. Grass ... moss ... weed ... then she felt the delicate, soft head of a closed flower. And more flowers. She peered closely and a jolt of hope shot through her.

She looked up at the sky. The breeze was blowing, but it was slight, and the blanket of cloud still hadn't shifted. "Come on," Nine hissed at the sky as she cradled the flower in her hand.

A bat swooshed above her and Nine instinctively ducked. The cloud was moving ... slowly ... slowly...

"COME ON!" Nine thumped the ground with her other hand. "Show yourself!"

A gust of strangely icy wind swept over Nine, who shuddered. She looked upwards. The cloud drifted away, revealing the moon. And it *was* the moon, except...

As Nine saw it, she felt a tightness spread across her chest. "Oh, how thoughtful your witch is," she muttered. Somehow, on the face of the moon, was the hexagonal clock from the hallway, glowing bright white. Three of the hands still whizzed backwards wildly and the smallest hand pointed at the 3.

Really no time to lose.

As the moonlight shone down, Nine moved her hand to the stalk, ready to snap it and –

Wait. A strange noise above the shrieking, sizzling, flapping chaos of the graveyard. Rustling? Not quite. Wriggling? That wasn't quite the word. Slithering? No…

Nine slowly turned around.

Dozens of vines had peeled away from the monument, raised up in the air, hovering, waiting – like deadly snakes ready to strike.

"I really, really hate magic," Nine squeaked.

Then the vines lurched towards her.

The vines coiled around Nine's satchel, tugging it, yanking it, and almost lifting her from her feet. "That – is – *mine!*" she roared, trying to tug it back.

The plant relinquished its grip, and Nine

stumbled back a step. She stood straight and proud and nodded sharply in their direction. That was … easy. Why was it so—

WHAM! She felt she'd been hit by a particularly nasty, heavy octopus as eight vines lashed out at her, grabbing her, wrapping around her. The graveyard turned upside down as Nine thrashed about in the air. Wriggling and tearing at the rough, rope-like vines did nothing. She was utterly powerless in their grip.

"Put me down, or else!" bellowed Nine, wondering when she'd last threatened a plant.

The vines suddenly released her in mid-air. Nine screamed as down she plummeted,

With one quick swoop, Nine threw out her hand to the ground, scooping up a sharp stone and a handful of damp earth. She held the stone like a dagger stabbing furiously, left and right, left and right, wincing as she caught her own arm in the fury – until down she fell with a thud on a bed of deadly nightshade.

"Make haste, Madam!" said a distant voice.

"Aye, and don't forget the flowers!"

Nine caught her breath as the graveyard still span around her. "This floaty red ball better be blimin' worth it," she muttered. Sitting up, she grabbed a handful of the flowers and stuffed them in her satchel. "I've got the flowers," Nine yelled. "I'm coming back!"

"Excellent news!" crowed the distant wizardy voice. As Nine turned towards the door, she looked up to see another bat hurtling towards her. Flapping – fluttering – *plop*! Sizzling droppings missed her face by an inch. Another plop to the right. And another.

Nine half ran, half staggered to the doorway where the troll, the wizard and the spoon were cheering her on. Deadly liquid rained down as she ran, echoing her own footsteps. She flapped wildly at the black shapes that flitted above her, focusing only on the doorway getting closer and closer...

"Come *on*, Madam!"

And closer and—

BOOM.

A strange ripple of energy rolled across the

graveyard. Nine stood perfectly still. Anything which felt BOOM-like was, she had learned, probably not a good thing. The bat was closing in when, suddenly, it vanished into nothing.

"Oh dear," said a not-so-crowing wizardy voice.

"Flabberghast?" she called, hoping he didn't hear the waver in her voice. Never. Show. Weak—

"I don't believe it's Wednesday any more."

"So it's Thursday? What – what happens on Thursday?" said Nine, still not daring to move.

"Monday dragon, Tuesday goblin, Wednesday bat…" rumbled Eric.

Her breathing quick and shallow, Nine slowly turned around. Her eyes widened as she saw the entire graveyard, as far as the eye could see, disappearing at an alarming rate. Gravestones and monuments were being swallowed up behind her, to the side of her, by a blackness – a complete nothingness.

"Thursday void," whimpered the troll.

"Oh no," murmured Nine.

"Run, lassie!"

Nine ran with legs that she couldn't feel on ground that wasn't there. Her breath was being sucked out. Her chest ached. There was no air. No light. No anything, except darkness that promised to stretch for ever – and she was going to become part of it.

Nothing. There was nothing. It was all over.

Life don't bring you…

CHAPTER 17

Nine was falling forwards without moving, pulled by something that wasn't there in a direction that didn't exist.

The back door slammed shut.

Nine felt as if she were waking from a dream. She gazed up at Eric, who was gripping her by the jacket. Nine pulled herself away dizzily and fell straight back down again.

"Never," she growled to Eric, "touch me again."

"Naughty Thursday," said Eric, his mouth downturned as Nine staggered to her feet.

"A marvellous success, Madam!" crowed Flabberghast, clapping his hands. "O-ho! That'll teach the witch!"

"You," said Nine, glaring at the wizard. "You knew that was going to happen. The void."

"Well you might not have gone out there in the first place if I'd told you. But never mind that now," said Flabberghast hastily.

"NEVER MIND?"

"The important thing, Madam, is that you have the flowers!"

"Lady hurt," said Eric, peering at her arm. He slowly, cautiously, reached out his long-nailed hand to examine a cut on Nine's arm.

Realising what he was doing, Nine quickly slapped it away. Eric gave a little whimper.

"Lady FINE," she said, only then realising how un-fine her arm was. Eric edged backwards and hung his head, and Nine felt a stab of shame. "Just get me a cloth or something," she muttered. "I'll sort it."

"Eric fetch." The troll lolloped off, his yellow dressing gown flapping behind him. Nine stumbled over to the kitchen table and collapsed into one of the chairs. The sugar bowl backed away a little.

"The nightshade, Madam," said Flabberghast, reaching his hand out. "There's no time to waste."

Feeling bruised and drained, Nine reached into her satchel, pulled out the flowers and pushed them towards Flabberghast. The wizard wiggled his fingers excitedly. "Splendid! Splendid!"

"Yes, you're welcome," Nine said grumpily.

Holding the precious flowers in one hand, Flabberghast stuck his head then his shoulders and then his entire body – as far as his slippers – into a small cupboard. He rummaged and clattered around inside.

"A-HA!" said a voice that sounded like it came from the other side of the House. Flabberghast reversed out of the tiny cupboard holding aloft a large mortar and pestle. "Victory shall be ours!"

"You know," Nine said loudly, "you are the most ridiculous wizard I have EVER met."

As Flabberghast began crushing the nightshade in the bowl, Eric sloped over to the table carrying a strip of white linen and a dish of water with a cloth. He placed the items down on the table then took a few steps backwards, twisting his tail. Nine looked at the wide-eyed troll and felt unfamiliar words burn her tongue. Words she could not speak. So she just said, "They'll do."

She waited until the troll stopped watching before dipping the cloth into the water and quickly bathing her arm. She awkwardly wrapped the linen bandage around the cut, but try as she could, she couldn't tie it up. She huffed in annoyance. The sugar bowl edged back another inch. Spoon jumped onto the table and, without a word, tied up the ends with his nimble, stick-like fingers. He paused for a second and looked Nine in the eyes. She stared back in wordless defiance.

"A-ha!" declared Flabberghast, pouring a jug of water over the crushed deadly nightshade in the mortar and giving it a stir. "The flowers are prepared. Madam, the letter!"

Nine pushed back her chair and dashed over to the TO DO board, driven by a new wave of energy. She tried to tug the letter free but the little jaws gave a rumbling growl and held it firm.

"How—?"

"Tickle under the chin!" called Flabberghast, as he marched towards the cauldron.

Nine lifted up the letter and tickled underneath the jaws. They released the letter into her hand, gave a little giggle, then melted back into the wooden board. The spoon jumped onto her shoulder as she reached the cauldron. Eric lolloped over towards them and gave a little whimper at the sight of his feather duster.

"Dear friends," Flabberghast began proudly as he held the mortar aloft, "the magic words are about to appear. The revenge curse will soon be broken! We shall not be shrunk beyond reality! Our freedom will be secured! My magic will be returned! And the toilet will be in the same place as we leave it!"

"By the way, I saw it on the fourth floor," said Spoon. "And it's grown teeth. Sit down very carefully."

"BEHOLD!" Flabberghast said as he tipped the mortar and poured the Revelato Potion over the items in the cauldron.

Everyone held their breath.

And held it.

And held it.

And held it…

Then, feeling slightly dizzy, there was a collective un-holding of breath. They all stared down at the letter. It still read '*so the magic words are…*'

"Nothing's happened!" Nine said, her heart thumping. Eric started whimpering.

Flabberghast tugged at his nightcap in frustration. "What?! We don't have time for this!" He dashed to the kitchen doorway then back to the cauldron. "The smallest clock hand is on the two!"

Flabberghast, Eric, Nine and Spoon all leaned closer over the cauldron and peered in…

BOOM! A powdery explosion of red surged out of the cauldron and they all staggered backwards. Spoon fell off Nine's shoulder. Eric looked into the cauldron and gave a wail of anguish. Still clutching the letter, Nine stepped forwards and, cautiously, followed his gaze. It was empty except for a few random sparks of red bouncing around inside the pot. Rage shot through every vein in Nine's body.

"Where's my music box?"

"Eric duster!" He grasped the cauldron with both hands, lifting it up to examine it thoroughly, above and below.

Flabberghast took a loud and quick intake of breath.

"The letter!" he hissed, jiggling on the spot. *"The magic words!"*

Nine looked down at the paper in her hand. Red, sparkling letters appeared one by one in a slow, swirly, deliberate style.

"S-O-N-G," read Nine. "W-I-N. W-A-R. *The magic words are: SONG WIN WAR.*"

She looked at Flabberghast. His eyes began changing to sparkly silver and a look of utter joy crept across his face. He thrust his fluffy, indigo-pyjamaed arms into the air. "I hereby break the revenge curse, oh Witch!" he said in what Nine presumed was supposed to be a deep, booming voice, but sounded more like he had a very sore throat. "SONG! WIN! WAR!"

Eric retracted his head from the cauldron and his eyes shifted nervously, left and right. Nine held her breath for a moment. Was … was that it? The jewel inside the floaty red ball was hers?

Flabberghast, his arms still outstretched, blinked a couple of times.

"The tea cupboard," he whispered to Nine. "Try it, Madam! Then we'll know if it's worked."

Nine ran over to the cupboard, her satchel bouncing on her hip, and touched the handle with her free hand.

ZAP! Eric disappeared in a puff of pink smoke. The spoon was an aardvark on a unicycle, which wobbled then fell with a crash on the floor. Nine felt herself split into four identical Nines standing in a row. Flabberghast was a purple donkey with – Nine felt a sickening lurch – Pockets' head. Instantly, one of the Nines raised her fists ready to fight. One Nine raised her arms to defend herself. Another Nine cautiously reached out a hand to him. And the real Nine gritted her teeth and refused to show anything. Pockets stared back, mouthed "No strawberries today" and grinned. Then a moment later he was gone and Flabberghast's face reappeared.

The magic faded and with a dizzy, melting feeling Nine fused back into one person. Flabberghast grabbed handfuls of his hair and dashed down the hall to look at the clock. Then he galloped back again, snatched the letter from Nine and read it furiously.

"Oi!" she snapped, snatching it back.

Flabberghast marched around the kitchen kicking every cupboard he could find. "I said your magic words!" he bellowed to the air. "What more do you want?"

"Witch clever," sighed Eric.

"All right. What exactly *was* your disagreement about?" asked Nine, feeling her patience trickle away to nothing. The wizard kicked the tall hat-stand in the corner. He yelped as the hat-stand sprouted a leg from nowhere and kicked him back.

"Come on! Think about what the magic words *mean*. Is there something else you're supposed to do?" Nine snapped. The wealth ... the escape...

No, no no! This was slipping through her fingers like another lost purse.

"SONG WIN WAR? They mean nothing to me!" shouted Flabberghast, rubbing his shin.

"That witch *is* clever," said Spoon.

"Will you all stop saying that!" roared Flabberghast in despair.

"Flabby?" Eric whimpered behind them in a slightly wobbly voice.

Flabberghast ignored the troll and threw his arms wide in despair. "We're doomed. Shrink into nothing. *Cease to exist.*" His eyes grew distant and unfocused. "I wonder if it's like growing backwards, but more painful. I bet she'll make it painful."

"Flabby?" came Eric's voice a little higher, a little wobblier.

Nine grasped hold of the wizard's arms and gave him a shake. "The words! THINK! I need that jewel!"

"Do you believe I am unaware of the severity of the situation? Oddly enough, I have no desire to cease existing! Breaking the curse is not about *you*, Madam. And I hardly think—"

"I've noticed!"

"FLABBY?" wailed Eric at the top of his voice.

"FLAB – BER – GHAST! Would three syllables actually kill you?!" snapped Flabberghast as he and Nine both whirled around irritably to face the troll.

"WHAT?!" bellowed Nine.

Eric twisted his tail and pointed to the witch's letter. The parchment was vibrating furiously, as if it was about to explode. Suddenly, all the words on the letter burst off the page and hurtled around the room in every direction.

"What!" cried Nine, flinching as the word 'fool' flew at her only to vanish right in front of her eyes. "What now?"

They stared at the blank parchment. Swirly scarlet writing appeared, each word flashing onto the page, then quickly fading:

'CATCH ME IF YOU CAN'

The parchment rose into the air, rolled itself into a long, thin, almost certainly unpleasant cylinder – and knocked Flabberghast's nightcap from his head. Then the parchment hurtled towards the arched door in the corner and slammed itself at the keyhole. Before anyone could move, it transformed into a long scroll the width of a pin, squeezed through the keyhole and disappeared.

"Oh no," said Flabberghast, placing his nightcap back on his head. "She hasn't."

"She flamin' has!" roared Spoon, drawing his sword from the sheath tied around his tartan pyjamas.

"So she's taken the parchment through the keyhole," said Nine, running over to the door and trying the handle. "Fine, we'll just unlock it and get it back. Come on, we need to get to…" She held her breath for a second, as the realisation hit her.

"The other side of this door." She turned around to face the others, who stood there, staring back doubtfully. "With the Sometimes…" Nine looked at Flabberghast and swallowed louder than she meant to. "…Dead."

"Indeed," said Flabberghast, with a warning tone. "And there's one more problem."

CHAPTER 18

"Oh no," Nine said, trying to keep her voice steady. "Tell me you have a key."

Flabberghast sighed loudly.

"The one door we need to get into RIGHT NOW," said Nine, feeling about to explode, "and there's no key?" Flabberghast covered his eyes with his hand and walked around in a circle. "But – but *why* is there no key?" said Nine, throwing her hands up in the air.

Flabberghast whirled around to face her. "If *you* had the Sometimes Dead living next door, I promise you, Madam, *you* would ensure there was no key as well!"

Eric began slamming his bulk against the

door. Spoon joined in, dodging occasionally to avoid being squished by the door-slamming troll.

"Sometimes – Sometimes – why are they *Sometimes* Dead?"

"Because, Madam," retorted Flabberghast, joining the others in throwing his weight against the door, "sometimes – they're – not!"

Nine stood and stared at the three inhabitants of this extraordinary and ridiculous House slamming their bodies repeatedly against the door. It didn't budge.

"Stop!" Nine said, "That isn't going to work!"

They kept on slamming into the door. In desperation, she went over to the tea cupboard and touched the handle.

ZAP! Nine was a clock, the hands whizzing backwards 3 – 2 – 1 – 15 – and the others—

A sick jolt hit Nine's stomach. Flabberghast, Eric and Spoon began to slowly shrink and shrink… Nine swallowed hard as the magic wore off and the three were restored to their normal size.

"Hitting the door is NOT going to work," she

said, trying to shake the image of shrinking from her head.

"Perhaps we speak the magic words into the keyhole!" said Flabberghast desperately. He bent down and put his mouth to the keyhole. "SONG WIN WAR!" he declared.

Without warning, the handle mutated into a human hand and grabbed the wizard's nose, holding him with a vice-like grip.

"Do something!" said Flabberghast, in a muted, nasal squeak. Spoon and Eric flew into action: the Spoon stabbing the fist; Eric trying and failing to prise open the fingers. But the handle-hand would not let go.

"Lassie!" cried Spoon. "You'd better have a trick up your sleeve."

Nine put her hand to her head. "There's no key for that door, no key… Is there another one that might work if we forced it?"

"No, Madam!" squeaked Flabberghast. "Of course there's not!"

Nine's eyes fell on *The Secret Book of Secrets and How to Uncover Them*, which sat silently, keeping its secrets on the table. She put the book to her mouth, glanced at the others, and whispered, "I really like Flabberghast's unicorn socks." She moved her face away quickly as the book sprung open. Hurriedly she turned to the contents page.

"There was something about keys," she said, scrolling her finger down the list. "Here! '*Enter Secret Places: How to Make a Skeleton Key*'!" Nine cried. "We need to make a skeleton key." She looked at the others. "What's a skeleton key?"

"One key, any lock," said Spoon. "I bought one from a dodgy elf once, when I needed to get my hands on some equipment."

"Well, hurry up," said Flabberghast, flapping his hands. "Go and fetch it."

"Nae, lad. Professor Dish has it now." His eyes darkened.

"Oh, how brilliant!" snapped Flabberghast, his eyes watering. "And why is there never a dodgy elf around when you need one?"

"A skeleton key!" said Nine as an idea flashed into her mind. "We don't need to make one. I reckon we've already got one."

"As usual, Madam, you make absolutely no sense!" squeaked Flabberghast.

But Nine dashed to the hallway staircase and ran up two steps at a time. On the landing, up the rickety staircase – to the closet. She yanked open the door and ran her eyes over the skeleton. What? Which bone would work? Was this completely beyond reason? Mind you, in *this* House, how could you tell?

"I'm ... you know…" She cleared her throat awkwardly, hating having to say this unfamiliar word, "*sorry* about this. I've got no choice. The witch is very clever."

She reached in and grabbed a bit of the skeleton's finger on the right hand. There was a sickening snapping sound. Nine grimaced. "Promise we'll bring it back."

"Of course, help yourself," rattled the skeleton, huffily, as Nine slammed the closet door shut. "Doesn't occur to anyone I might *want* my finger!"

Nine ran back along the landing, satchel bouncing.

"Or be brought out for a nice change of scene!"

boomed the skeleton after her. "Perhaps have my ribs dusted…"

Nine dashed back down the rickety staircase and the plum-carpeted steps, trying not to think about rib-dusting. She glanced at the clock as she ran past and was flooded by a sensation of almost unbearable panic. The smallest hand was heading past the 1, back up to the 15 at the top. No! She was so close – *so close* – to getting the jewel!

As she entered the kitchen, she saw Eric wringing his tail and the spoon standing on Flabberghast's head, desperately trying to pull his sword out of the handle's knuckle. Nine poked the finger bone into the lock and wiggled it left and right. *Come on.* Left and right. *COME ON!*

CLUNK! The handle-hand released Flabberghast's nose so quickly and violently that he staggered backwards and landed bottom-first in the bucket of orange ceiling slime.

"Will someone *please* empty that bucket?!" Flabberghast shouted as he quickly pulled himself up. The handle-hand transformed back into a handle, sending Spoon and his sword flying through the air and crashing back into Flabberghast, making him lose his balance and land in the bucket. Again.

Flabberghast rubbed his nose and looked at Nine. She tucked the finger bone key into her satchel and stared back at him.

"Nearly on the fifteen," she said. "We're going in." Cautiously she put her hand on the handle. Then, when it didn't attempt to grab her face, she turned it and pushed. The door was heavier and stiffer than she expected but back it went, scraping a little on the stone step.

"The door was locked long ago by my great-great-great-grandfather. I was told as a child never to open it. I'd stake my best nightcap that's exactly why the witch has made us open it."

"Quite probably," said Nine, trying to peer into the darkness.

"We die?" whimpered Eric.

"Quite probably," growled Spoon, hopping onto Nine's shoulder.

Nine crept onto the stone step on the other side of the door. Whatever was down there wasn't going to be a bowl of strawberries…

"Come on," she whispered and began to slowly tiptoe down the stone steps, grateful for the light coming from the kitchen behind them. Flabberghast and Eric followed behind as they edged down the spiral staircase. Nine rested one hand against the wall, feeling the cold, uneven stone on her skin. The air was cold as the grave.

"At least we can always get out if we need to," muttered Flabberghast.

Nine glanced up at the doorway, almost obscured by Eric's form on the stairs. She could always get out … get out of the House if she needed to. She could run for it. Should she run for it? Forget the jewel, forget freedom…

Out of nowhere, a familiar icy breeze whooshed up towards them from below, passing through Nine's body like a freezing blade, before it dashed up the stone steps, out of the door and—

SLAM. Blackness. Last chance gone.

"I really think you should stop talking," hissed

Nine as a cold, sick feeling settled in her chest. An indignant huff came from behind.

Suddenly Flabberghast bumped into Nine, almost overbalancing her. Her heart shot into her mouth as Spoon clung onto her neck. Nine caught her balance and took a deep breath.

"Oops," said a sorry-sounding troll voice behind them.

"Watch your step!" hissed Spoon.

"Shhh!" whispered Nine and Flabberghast.

The next second Nine was shoved violently forward, losing her footing. She flung out her arms as she tumbled down the steps and came to a thumping halt on damp, stony ground with a wizard's knee in her back and a spoon in her ear. A large force then rolled into them all.

"More oops," said the large force, which sounded a lot like Eric.

They scrambled to their feet. In the pitch black, Nine could sense Flabberghast standing up in front of her. She jumped a little as she felt the spoon land on her shoulder again. She stretched out her arms sideways and felt the damp, cold walls of…

"A tunnel?" she whispered as they edged forwards in darkness.

"Just a short passage down to the crypt—" Flabberghast stopped talking. And moving. With a soft thud, Nine walked into him. With a hard thud, Eric walked into Nine. Instinctively she caught the spoon as he flew off her shoulder.

"What is it?" she hissed to the wizard.

Flabberghast made a loud gulping sound and then continued to creep forward. "Ohhhh dear. I have a terrible feeling … it is just remotely possible … I may have made a slight … miscalculation."

"You'd better not have done, laddie," said Spoon. "Ask any scientist. Miscalculations can be deadly!"

But Flabberghast said nothing. Nine felt him creep forward more slowly than before. Suddenly the walls of the passage opened up. They all huddled together in the darkness.

Silence. Still silence. Unbearable, doom-bringing silence.

"Now what?" whispered Flabberghast.

"I don't know, do I?" hissed Nine.

"Well, think of something!"

"In case you hadn't realised, I'm not actually an expert in this curse-breaking business!"

"Fear not, Madam," hissed Flabberghast, "I reached that conclusion long ago."

"Are you two quite finished?" came a clear, strong female voice. A voice that Nine recognised.

The witch: she was here. Nine's heart leapt to her throat and Flabberghast drew in a sharp breath.

"I mean, I hate to interrupt you, really I do," continued the voice, "just, I thought there was a more pressing matter to which to attend. Apart from anything else, the residents down here seem rather … restless."

Nine could feel Flabberghast and Eric edging closer to her and she fought back the instinct to say "Don't touch". There was the sound of someone clicking their fingers and then a whooshing roar of flame as wall-mounted wooden torches burst into light all around the room.

They were standing in a crypt with vaulted stone arches stretching across the ceiling. Elabo-rately carved thick pillars lined the crypt on each side. Dotted around beside these pillars were nine tombs with a stone effigy of a figure carved on each top. Facing them at the end of the room was a white marble statue of a queen sitting on a throne, wielding a sword in one hand and a set of scales in the other.

"Ohhhh dear," said Flabberghast, edging closer to Eric.

Without warning, the stone queen stood up from her throne. Nine gasped and stepped backwards. The statue began to shake more and more violently.

"What –" began Nine.

"– the –" said Spoon.

"Devil?" said Flabberghast.

Suddenly, the white marble exploded. Nine and the others shielded their eyes and ducked as showers of pale stone flew towards them. They looked up to see the witch, with her silky tumble of red hair and elaborate black crinoline dress, standing in the crypt, looking right at them.

Because this time, she had a face.

She seemed only a few years older than Nine

but had piercing blue eyes that looked as strangely ancient and deep as the sea, and there was something else about her face that was familiar, but Nine couldn't put her finger on it…

Flabberghast gulped extremely loudly.

"Hello, Flabberghast," said the witch in her dangerously smooth voice. She cocked her head slightly to one side, smiled sweetly and widened her eyes. "Let's play!"

CHAPTER 19

Flabberghast immediately turned for the staircase.

"Uh-uh-uh..." sang the witch, waggling her finger in the air. Strands of red lightning shot out from her fingertips, stretched across to Flabberghast and grabbed hold of him. He froze mid-dash. The witch turned her outstretched hands palm up and slowly wiggled her fingers. The red lightning forced Flabberghast to turn around against his will. His terrified eyes stared at her.

"You. Who *are* you?" demanded Nine, her mouth dry and her heart thumping.

"Who am I? You mean he hasn't told you?"

said the witch, giving Flabberghast a look of disapproval. She tutted. "I'm his sister."

"Of course! It's the nose!" said Nine, looking at the witch's flared nostrils. "*That's* what looks familiar." Then another thought struck her as she looked from the witch to Flabberghast. *Good grief. There's two of them.*

Things started to make sense. The disagreement between the witch and Flabberghast ... the way she knew his worst fears... "But what is it that you want?" said Nine.

The witch smiled sweetly again. "Revenge."

"For what exactly?" said Nine, cautiously.

"This ridiculous excuse for a wizard turned my hair pink for Auntie Griselda the Unruly's wedding. I detest pink!"

"Well, she cursed my hopscotch robes!" said Flabberghast, "in the middle of the championships! Every time I hopped I turned into a rabbit!"

The witch let out a shrill, tinkly laugh then stopped suddenly and narrowed her eyes. "He turned my pet dragon into a toy and then made him vanish!"

"She froze me in time for a week – I missed my own birthday!"

Nine stared at them in disbelief. "A squabble. This is about a *squabble*?"

"He BANISHED me from this House!"

"It was only going to be until you apologised—"

"*Me* apologise?" laughed the witch. "You didn't even do the spell terribly well, dearest. You cast it over the House but forgot to include the crypt in the banishment!"

"A *slight* miscalculation! I just forgot to include anything below ground!"

"I realised your unbelievable stupidity when I delivered the letter yesterday. Strolling round the outside of the House, for old times' sake," she sighed dramatically. "There was a break in the magic, right around the back door to the crypt. Did you forget about that, dearest? Down the stone steps underground?"

Flabberghast grimaced. "But it was still a charm of immense complexity!"

"Oh yes," said the witch, her voice becoming smooth. Dangerously smooth. "And now, brother dearest, do tell them what you said through the letterbox after you banished me. Tell them why I cursed this House."

Flabberghast tightened his lips and said nothing.

"No?" said the witch. She twisted her wrist and pointed at Flabberghast's leg. A red light zapped out from her fingers, striking Flabberghast on the shin. He yelped and bent over, rubbing his leg. Without looking, Eric hoisted the wizard back into an upright position.

"Ah, maybe some games will loosen your tongue," said the witch, strutting backwards and forwards across the stone flooring. The sound of her boot heels echoed around them. "I love games."

"Never would have guessed," said Nine.

The witch smiled at her, showing a row of perfect white teeth. "You. Yes, you. You've done quite well to get so far," she said. "With your brainless troll, your kitchen utensil and your pathetic excuse for a wizard."

"They are not 'mine'," Nine said, but the

witch just smiled knowingly then looked at Flabberghast.

"And fancy you having *friends*. I thought I was the only one who would put up with you!"

Flabberghast glared at her as the witch sauntered on. She stopped in front of Nine and stared intensely at her. Nine shifted uncomfortably but held her ground, staring back, digging her nails into her clenched fists. The witch looked at her with a mix of curiosity and pity, then leaned forward and put her mouth to Nine's ear.

"Still no strawberries?" she whispered. Nine gasped and momentarily unclenched her fists. She stared at the witch, who strutted back to the middle of the crypt.

"Too much talking, not enough playing," sang the witch impatiently. She reached both hands above her head as if she were holding an imaginary sphere. The gap between her hands took the form of the glowing not-a-moon – the hexagonal clock. The three hands whizzed round and the small sword hand was nearly back at the 15. She threw it upwards, where it hovered in mid-air.

"Oh and look: you're so nearly out of time. I wonder what it will feel like, being shrunk out of existence. Squishy, I suppose."

"The Revenge Curse should be broken!" said Flabberghast as his sister strutted around the crypt, poking the stone effigies on top of the tombs. "We made our sacrifices. I said the magic words!"

The witch span around to face him. "The magic words?" She tapped her cheek thoughtfully with a long, perfect nail and smiled. "Oh! Brother dear, I'm disappointed in you. Surely you don't think *these* are the magic words, do you?"

She raised her hand in the air and twisted her fingers into a closed fist. The parchment appeared again. *'The magic words are*: SONG WIN WAR', then it crumbled to dust and dropped to the floor, leaving just the red, sparkling letters hanging in mid-air. Nine eyed the witch cautiously.

"How decidedly dull. Where is the fun in telling you the exact words?"

"But—" began Nine, then she stopped. Because there was a sudden, stony grinding sound.

"The Sometimes Dead!" whispered Flabber-ghast. "I think they're doing the Sometimes Not Dead bit."

Eric whimpered and began rummaging in his dressing-gown pocket for sweets. Spoon pointed his sword around the crypt. Nine watched in horror as, one by one, each of the nine stone effigies seemed to come to life, sliding slowly from the top of their tombs and standing on two definitely Not Dead legs. Their stone eyes rolled backwards and two solid, cloudy-blue ovals sat in their place. Their noses all had the same flared nostrils.

"Who are they?" said Nine as every muscle in her body tensed.

"Distant relatives from our family tree," said Flabberghast. "There's Marvin the Merciless. That one with the dagger is Agatha the Rather Short-Tempered. Millicent the Goat-Eater with the sword. And that's Sybil the Particularly Fond of Biting and—"

"Biting?!" said Nine.

The witch gave a little cry of satisfaction. "Oh, I adore family reunions! Did anyone bring

193

sandwiches?" She stepped away from the clock, which remained glowing in the air. "Three minutes to go, Flabberghast. Perhaps we should … liven things up a little." She began to skip in a circle around Nine and the others.

"Oh no. Not skipping," murmured Flabberghast. "It never ends well when there's skipping."

Nine twisted her head, watching for any moment of explosive trickery. Something was coming…

The witch skipped around them, pointing to the glowing clock and singing:

"Girls and boys come up to play,

The moon doth shine as bright as day.

Leave your supper and leave your room,

And join your playfellow –"

She stopped and smiled darkly at them.

"– IN THE TOMB!"

The witch twisted her hands again, then thrust them out to the sides. Each of the red, sparkling letters flew towards a Sometimes Dead, Sometimes Not person and burned itself into their stone chests. Their bright blue oval eyes instantly turned red. The witch smiled. There was a united stony stomp as all the figures took a step towards Nine and the others – all the figures except one, which held a long, stone staff.

"Ignatius the Permanently Late!" said Flabberghast. There was a little solitary stomp as the staff-bearing statue took a step to catch up with the others.

"Come, come, don't be shy," said the witch, skipping around the statues and twisting her fingers in a sharp motion. The figures took another step forward. Ignatius took another step forward. With a stiff, grinding sound, Sybil the Particularly Fond of Biting opened her jaws unnaturally wide to reveal sharp, stony teeth. Marvin the Merciless raised his sword. Agatha the Rather Short-Tempered raised a dagger.

The witch moved behind Sybil, who lifted her hands in a throat-gripping motion.

"I know, Auntie Sybil," she said, "he does rather have that effect on people." Another stony stomp echoed through the crypt. Another solitary step echoed after.

"So what stops the Sometimes Dead from being Sometimes *Not* Dead?" asked Nine, edging closer to the others.

"Er – what?" said Flabberghast.

"WHAT MAKES THEM STOP TRYING TO KILL US?" shouted Nine.

"Oh! I believe at some point they simply get bored of being alive again and go back to being dead. Of course, that was before they had –" Flabberghast glared at the witch – "PURE EVIL IN A DRESS controlling them."

The witch smiled sweetly and pointed at Flabberghast. A jet of red light shot out of her finger disintegrating Flabberghast's nightcap into little flakes of ash that floated mournfully to the stone floor.

"Oi!" Flabbergast snapped. "I liked that nightcap!"

"Old-fashioned, tatty and barely suitable for purpose," said the witch airily. "Yes, it suited you so well, brother dear."

"I say we take them on," said Spoon.

"Nine stone statues. Three idiots and me. No

chance," said Nine. "Your sword would end up blunter than Eric's sentences."

"Eric sentence?" said Eric, puzzled.

Flabberghast looked around. "What do you want from us? What do you want us to do?" he called out angrily.

"You know what you need to do to break the curse, Flabberghast," the witch's voice oozed silkily through the air. She stepped out from behind one of the pillars and stepped back again. Then she appeared from behind the pillar opposite. "What you've always had to do." She disappeared behind the pillar again.

Then they all startled as a voice behind them hissed, "Say the magic words."

By the time they had turned around to look at the witch, she had gone again. Nine looked rapidly at all the pillars – behind them – above them: where was she? What was her next move? As if in reply, a soft red glow appeared at the end of the room. It faded away to reveal the witch sitting sideways on the stone throne, her legs kicked lazily over the side.

"You've only ever had to say the magic words," said the witch. She clicked her fingers and the statues took three steps forward. Ignatius caught up.

Nine, Spoon and Eric all turned to look at Flabberghast, who looked flabbergasted. "SONG WIN WAR! *I've said the magic words*."

"Oh Flabberghast. Do use your brain, dearest. I know it hurts."

"Well?" demanded Nine, turning to Flabberghast. "If those aren't the magic words, what are?"

"I – do – not – know!" he said, pulling at his hair.

"Shame," said the witch, examining a fingernail. The Sometimes Dead all took another step closer and formed a line, closing ranks.

"Enough nonsense!" Spoon hollered and leapt towards Ignatius the Permanently Late. Without turning its head the statue raised its free hand, caught the spoon in mid-air and clasped its stony fist shut around him. Spoon's little sword tinkled to the ground and his spindly legs kicked wildly in mid-air. "Put me down! I'll have your head for this!"

"Say the magic words, Flabberghast," the witch sang, swinging her booted legs carelessly.

"But I don't KNOW—"

"Getting *bored* now," sang the witch with a sharp edge in her voice. She waved her hand carelessly and the statues all stepped towards them and didn't stop. Ignatius the Permanently Late stamped his staff on the stone floor a moment after. Dust and fragments of stone rained down on them from the ceiling.

"She really is going to kill us," coughed Flabberghast. "What do we do?!"

The statues stepped forwards. Ignatius stepped forwards. Nine, Eric and Flabberghast backed away until, with an unwelcoming thump, they felt the damp chill of the subterranean stone wall on their backs. There was nowhere else to go. Nine's eyes widened as the statues aimed their swords, daggers and staffs right at them. Sybil licked her lips with a stony tongue.

"Song win war. Song win war," muttered Flabberghast quickly. "What – what – do you want me to sing?"

"Heavens, no," called the witch from the throne. "You're always off-key. Now tick tock, tick tock, you're nearly out of time, Flabberghast."

Nine glanced at the clock, still hovering in mid-air. There was a hair's breadth before it hit 15. Still on the throne the witch stretched out her arms, and her hands formed into twisted claw-like shapes, the fingertips glowing glittery red. She flicked her hand towards Marvin the Merciless. In a heartbeat, the statue reached forward, grabbed Flabberghast, twisted him around to face the others and pinned his sword across Flabberghast's throat.

"Stop it!" hissed the wizard.

"And spoil the fun?" said the witch coolly.

Agatha the Rather Short-Tempered pointed her stone dagger towards Nine, ready to strike. Suddenly, Eric let out a roar of panic and dashed forwards, shielding Nine from the statue. But a click of fingers came from the other end of the crypt. Red sparks shot from the witch's hand…

…and Eric froze.

CHAPTER 20

Eric's long-nailed feet turned to the mottled grey stone of the statue, then his legs, his stomach – then Nine gasped, as with one last, desperate action, the Nearly Completely Sometimes Dead troll looked at Nine and reached into his dressing-gown pocket. As he threw the boiled sweets into the air towards Nine, his arm and the sweets turned to stone. Nine stared at them, just hanging in the air in front of her face. She looked at the Completely Sometimes Dead troll and then at the witch.

She took a deep breath and an ocean of rage rose up inside her. "HOW DARE YOU?" she bellowed.

"Oh, quite easily," called the witch. "Don't tell me you liked him … did you?"

"Turn him back at once!" demanded Flabberghast.

"Hmmmmmmmmmmm… No."

The rage in Nine exploded and she went to charge at the witch, but Millicent the Goat-Eater marched towards her, sword in hand. Nine retreated, her back against the wall. She gasped as the Not Dead Millicent pointed her sword at Nine's heart. Nine's breaths came quick and fast.

Focus. She needed to focus.

She stared at the red letters on all the statues. Now the letters and words were all mixed up… Three of the statues now read S-A-W…

That's it!

"The exact words!" she yelled. "She didn't give us the exact words. She gave us the letters! It isn't SONG WIN WAR, it's the *letters* in the words! We need to make different magic words!"

From the throne came slow clapping. "You know, Flabberghast, she's really rather good." Her eyes met Nine's. "However did you find her?"

Then, with a noisy swish of crinoline, she swung her legs dramatically back around, bouncing out of the throne. "But then you love your words and your books, don't you?" Her eyes flashed red just like the eye at the library.

Nine looked desperately from statue to statue. She mustn't get distracted. Don't think about the glowing red eyes. Don't think about the cold wall at her back. Don't think about the sword at her heart. Don't think about Eric...

Focus! The letters.

"I RAN – I GO – IN GO –"

The witch twisted her fingers lazily and Sybil the Particularly Fond of Biting walked towards Nine. She slowly put her head on one side and widened her jaws even further.

"Stop! Be reasonable!" Flabberghast bellowed at the witch. Marvin's sword edged closer to his throat.

"Reasonable?" oozed the witch, tossing her scarlet hair over her shoulder. "Do you consider banishing someone from their own House *reasonable*, dearest?"

"You utterly deserved to be locked out! And I left your suitcase outside, made sure Aunt Griselda knew to expect you—"

"While you popped off in the House and did a spot of friend-shopping!" The witch looked disapprovingly at Eric and Spoon.

"I would have let you back in … eventually. But when I came back, you cast this wretched curse on the House before I could lift mine and—"

"Ha!" crowed the witch. "Yes, this curse! Oh, banishment is nothing compared to this! Is it? IS IT?!" The witch threw her arms up in the air and turned around slowly on the spot, clearly relishing every second. "This wonderful, beautiful curse I have created! Ooooh, I'm so glad you banished me. This has been … delightful!"

She smiled sweetly at Flabberghast. "Are you sure you don't want to tell them what you said through the letterbox?"

Focus. Nine stared at all the letters in desperation. "I SAW…?"

"Ooh!" squealed the witch. "Tick tock – watch

204

the clock. Oh, how time *does* fly when you're having fun. Are you having fun?"

Nine looked up at the clockface. The smallest sword hand was about to hit 15.

"Say the magic words, brother dear! LOUD AND CLEAR. You have four seconds until the shrinking begins. That's if our relatives don't kill you first." She sighed. "Every family reunion's the same."

"I don't KNOW the words!" cried Flabberghast as Marvin's dagger pushed a little harder against his throat. Sybil the Particularly Fond of Biting gnashed her stony teeth together and leaned towards Nine's neck. Millicent's stony sword slid up towards her throat.

"I SANG – I WAS –" said Nine desperately. "I WAS –"

"Ooh, it's all so terribly exciting," said the witch, her dress swishing as she strutted. "Terribly." She stared coolly at Nine and pointed her finger.

"WRONG!" shouted Nine.

A red light shot out of the witch's finger. Nine felt a sharp chill in her heart. Then a cold, heavy feeling hit her feet and started to spread up her legs. She looked down. Stone.

"I beg your pardon?" said the witch, stopping where she stood.

"I ... WAS ... WRONG!" The cold, heavy feeling spread up Nine's legs. "The words ... Flabberghast!"

"Say them!" yelled Spoon, still wriggling in Ignatius' grasp.

"And mean them!" gasped Nine breathlessly.

The witch stared at Nine and a ghost of a smile flickered across her face. The stone swept up Nine's body, spread heavily over her heart, crept up her neck – her jaw –

Flabberghast let out a roar of frustration. "I –" he bellowed – "WAS – WRONG!"

The witch let out a victorious whoop of delight and hovered up in the air, raising her arms in triumph. The not-a-moon clock smashed noisily and shards flew across the crypt, fading into nothing. Nine felt the cold stone melt away and warmth return to her body. She breathed a sigh of relief, then looked at Eric and saw his stone body turn back to furry flesh. With a little clatter, all the sweets fell to the ground.

"Drop sweets," he said sadly, looking at them in confusion. Nine hesitated then bent down and picked one up. Without meeting the troll's gaze, she pushed it into his hand.

The eyes of the statues returned to their cloudy blue. They glanced around, looking a little lost. Ignatius the Permanently Late held up Spoon to eye level and tilted his head on one side as if to ponder why he was holding a leg-thrashing murderous utensil and if this was really a good idea.

He dropped Spoon on the floor and yawned. The statues all stomped back to their tombs, lying back down on their lids, until only Ignatius the Permanently Late had a last look around before sloping back to his resting place.

"There!" said the witch shrilly, landing on the ground before Flabberghast. "That wasn't so hard, was it, brother dear? You should have told them what you said through the letterbox. They would have solved it instantly!"

"I *really* don't like you any more," Flabberghast growled. "You could have killed us!"

"Oh, just a little excitement, Flabberghast. You really are as dreary as this old House. Auntie Griselda the Unruly is much more fun!"

"So that – that's it?" flustered the wizard. "My powers are back?"

"Yes, yes," said the witch in a bored tone, "your powers – if you could call them that – are back."

Flabberghast made a rapid twisting movement with his hands, as if he was undoing the lid of a jar. Silver sparks shot out and he yelled in delight.

"And as for your pathetic sacrifices," said the witch. "I suggest you try the cupboard under the stairs." Flabberghast groaned. "*Amazing* what you have in the cupboard under the stairs," she added in a voice that could cut stone.

Flabberghast froze for a moment then looked at her out of the corner of his eye. "Ah," he said.

"Oh, and I suppose you want this back too," said the witch.

She twisted her hands and the red floating ball appeared. She twisted her fingers again and the ball floated towards the wizard, stopping and hovering right in front of his face. Nine stared, her heart in her mouth. This was it… The witch clicked her fingers and the red glow faded to nothing, and something blue and silver plummeted to the ground and landed with a tinkling sound at the wizard's feet.

"The jewel!" said Nine eagerly, diving to collect it from the floor.

"Ugly-looking thing," said the witch as she pulled a face. She glanced at Flabberghast. "I don't know why mother bothered to leave it to you and not me."

Flabberghast scowled at the witch but Nine ran her fingers over the jewel and smiled. A large sapphire set inside a silver oval. Undoubtedly worth a fortune. Words were engraved in strange runes in the silver. She looked up at Flabberghast.

"What does it say?"

Flabberghast cleared his throat and cast a glance at the witch. "'From dung we reach for stars'," he whispered as the witch raised an eyebrow. "Family motto."

Nine twisted her mouth doubtfully. "No one need know about that," she said.

"Moving on," said Flabberghast, straightening himself up. "Now, I presume the toad's tongue is back? The House can move? The pictures are straight? The curse is truly broken?"

"Yes, the curse is broken," said the witch in a bored tone. "Weeeeeeell…" She gave a tiny shrug. "More or less."

"More or less?" said Flabberghast, freezing. "More or – what do you mean '*MORE OR LESS*'?"

"It's just possible," said the witch lazily, stretching her arms by her sides and giving her fingers a playful wiggle, "that you may find the odd thing here or there not quite to your absurdly high level of satisfaction. I'm sure you'll adapt. Eventually."

She began to strut away then paused and called over her shoulder. "Lovely to see you again, brother dear. Enjoy your tea." She looked at Nine out of the corner of her eye and gave a half-smile.

For the briefest of moments, her black crinoline dress changed into the scarlet dress of the young lady at the market. Nine gasped. Then the witch gave Flabberghast a smug look and held her hand in the air. She twisted her wrist sharply and the oversized woollen dragon from the cupboard under the stairs fell from nowhere. The witch reached out her arm to catch it and as she did…

A flash of green scales – a flap of wing – a blur of scarlet – and the witch vanished leaving behind only red sparks in the outline of a dragon with its wings outstretched. They fell and faded to nothing.

"Was that – did she – did that just turn into a REAL DRAGON?" asked Nine, staring as the last sparks disappeared. She turned to look at Flabberghast but he had a vague, dreamy expression on his pale face.

"Tea," he whispered, and ran towards the steps.

Nine couldn't resist a smile. "Freedom," she whispered, and tucked the jewel into her satchel.

CHAPTER 21

Giving a skeleton back his finger was not something Nine ever expected to do. Yet here she was, pushing it into his hand where a strange force clicked it back into place.

"There you go," she said. She gave the skeleton one last look, wondering who he had been – or possibly still was – why he was in a closet and why Flabberghast had become so flustered when she had mentioned him... But there wasn't time for chit-chat with a bunch of bones so she shut the wardrobe door and said, "I need to go now. Goodbye, Bonehead."

"That's a shame," boomed the skeleton's voice as she made her way down the stairs. "We were rather getting on. Apart from you stealing my finger, of course."

As she turned into the hallway, Nine saw Flabberghast wading through, and wobbling over, a humongous pile of clutter which had spilled out from the cupboard under the stairs. He was holding a kilt (now decorated with pink ribbons), a feather duster (which had been given a haircut) and his hopscotch trophy.

"Evil, evil witch!" Flabberghast screeched, holding up his trophy. "Look at it!"

Nine looked at the trophy. *"WORLD HOPSCOTCH CHAMPION, eighteen—"*

"The name!"

Nine snorted. "Flabby!"

"I despise her," he said, kicking the Vampire Starter Kit back into the cupboard.

"Oh, I don't know," said Nine with an inkling of what might have been described as respect. "I think I'm warming to her."

Then Nine's heart skipped a beat. There was something silver, something familiar, poking out underneath the InkFree quill and a piece of parchment. She swallowed hard.

Her music box. Her beautiful, beautiful music box.

Nine scooped it up and held it close to her chest. She took a deep, silent breath as she blinked back that horrible burning feeling in her eyes again. She looked up anxiously, hoping Flabberghast hadn't noticed, but he was busy trying to shake his purple slipper free from the troll-sized pants. Nine couldn't help but smile at Flabberghast's exasperation as both the pants and the slipper went flying off back into the cupboard.

She tucked the music box into her satchel and then, out of curiosity, reached down for the InkFree quill. It looked normal enough for something magical. She picked up the parchment and as Flabberghast clambered over the clutter and retrieved his slipper, she began to write a short note – whatever came straight into her head. The ink flowed freely. The words flowed freely. Nine stared at what she had written, the secret, special words that came from the heart. She stared at the note and sighed.

No. She went to screw up the parchment into a ball then stopped. Instead she folded it and stuffed it hastily into her satchel.

"Maybe magic's not so bad after all," she said, examining the quill. "Can I keep this?"

"As you wish, Madam," grumbled Flabberghast, trying to shove the Complete Family Set of Pop-Up Coffins back into the cupboard. They popped up in his face.

Nine put the quill in her satchel and glanced at the front door. She could leave right now. Take the jewel and go. Start the rest of her life. Then she heard a clatter of crockery from the kitchen. Maybe just one moment more together... Nine stepped over a pop-up coffin and headed down the hallway.

The kettle was boiling on the stove and Eric, wearing his frilly apron over his dressing gown, was preparing the tea set. Flabberghast walked into the kitchen.

"Well I propose the tidying waits until after a cup of tea. The toad's tongue is back and the pictures are straight!" He put the kilt on the table and handed Eric his feather duster.

"Best duster!" said Eric, cuddling it.

"I believe this is a moment for celebration," said Flabberghast.

Nine thought about the pictures for a moment. "So," she said, "Horatio the Untidy, Millicent the Goat-Eater… Come on, what *is* your title? Flabberghast the what?"

"Flabberghast the … Magnificent," the wizard said, drawing himself as tall as he could.

Nine snorted. "I don't believe that for a second."

Flabberghast ignored her. "Dr Spoon is just locating the toilet. Now … tea." He moved to the tea cupboard, wiggling his sparkling fingers in anticipation. Eric plonked the teacups onto the table and smiled a wonky smile at Nine.

"Just before I go," said Nine, "I have a question." So, so many questions… But mainly she wanted the answer to one. "What were you wrong about?" she asked, looking closely at Flabberghast.

"The disagreement we had, it just … er … got out of hand…" muttered the wizard.

"Out of hand?!" said Nine. "She tried to kill us! Come on, what were you wrong about? What did you say to her through the letterbox?

Flabberghast shifted awkwardly from foot to foot then gave a huge sigh of resignation. "I said … I said my *mumblemumblemumble*."

"Louder," said Nine.

"I said – I said my powers were superior to hers."

Eric let out a guffaw at the same time as Nine nearly burst herself with a sudden explosion of laughter. Flabberghast tutted and huffed at them both and reached for the handle of the tea cupboard, a look of love and desire on his face. He touched the handle—

ZAP. Still holding the cupboard's handle, but opening the door towards him, Flabberghast had an accordion for a face with two huge eyes blinking in surprise in the middle. Eric was a frilly-apron-wearing frog with a pink top hat. Nine was a big bubble with a satchel. She felt herself getting bigger and bigger until…

POP! Nine was herself again. "I think we've found one of the things which isn't 'quite up to your absurdly high level of satisfaction'."

Flabberghast reached inside the cupboard. "Well, it's a small price to pay for tea." He opened the lid of a tin caddy and let out a sigh of delight. He waltzed over to Eric, who spooned some tea into the clean teapot.

"You refused to say it, so she got you to finally admit it in front of everyone," said Nine, unable to resist smiling.

"I only said that to break the curse," said Flabberghast, his cheeks turning slightly pink. "Of course, it's not actually true. I was *not* wrong. Truly my powers are superior to hers."

Spoon marched into the room, jumped up on the table and examined his kilt. "You know, I found the toilet again, lad. It's in your bedroom now, stuck to the ceiling."

"Stuck?" said Flabberghast.

"Aye. Upside down."

"Upside down?!" said Flabberghast, his mouth dropping open.

"Right above your bed."

"Above my—? That … *witch*!" Flabberghast roared to the room.

Nine exploded with another snort of laughter. "Flabberghast, her powers are *definitely* superior to yours."

"Apparently so," said the wizard tightly as he sank down in one of the kitchen chairs.

Eric poured the tea – three normal cups and a tiny thimble for Spoon, before sitting down clumsily.

"Before you go, Madam?" said Flabberghast, holding out a cup. "It's the finest tea in all the realms."

Nine looked at the front door. "Just a mouthful. I need to take this jewel to a shop." They all looked at their cups, picked them up simultaneously and raised them in a silent, exhausted toast. Then they took a mouthful.

As the smooth, warm liquid went down her throat, Nine's whole body felt refreshed. It seemed to spread to every part of her. She no longer felt like she had narrowly avoided being sizzled alive by putrid droppings, crushed by an enchanted cupboard, nearly suffocated by evil vines and almost turned into a Nearly Completely

Sometimes Dead statue while trying to outwit a fiend of a witch who was clearly rather smart.

For one moment, as she drank that tea in silence, in the strangest kitchen in the world, everything felt … perfectly fine.

"What flavour is that?" said Nine, licking her lips.

"Strawberry tea," sighed Flabberghast blissfully. "Isn't it wonderful?"

"Strawberry tea," Nine said, staring at the cup. "It's all right, I suppose," she shrugged, clanging her cup back on the saucer. She forced away a smirk at the look of utter bliss on the faces of her companions.

"More tea," said Eric and filled her cup.

Before she knew it, the oddest tea party in history had lasted hours and many cups of tea had been drained. Nine didn't know what the time was exactly but guessed the pawn shop would be opening soon. She could move on with the rest of her life.

She put her cup down onto the saucer and paused as Pockets' face sprang into her mind. She felt an uncomfortable mixture of hate and pity. She looked at her strange tea companions. Pockets had never known anything like this…

"I owe someone a gift," she said. "Can I take some of that tea? It might put him in a better mood."

Flabberghast nodded and looked at her. "Be my guest, Madam."

Nine hesitated for a moment as the words hung in the air. Flabberghast filled a little purple tin with some tea leaves and handed it to Nine.

"He'll like that," she said stiffly, staring at the tin longer than she needed to. "Right, I'm going."

"As are we, Madam," said Flabberghast, rubbing his eyes. "We will not trouble you again. Once you have left, we shall move on. We like to travel the worlds, and the worlds between the worlds. The House is unpredictable and full of adventure in itself – there are rooms even I know little about – but it's rather pleasant for the House to take us on a trip. The freedom makes one feel rather alive."

"Aye," said Spoon, stifling a yawn, "and we've a Dish to find."

Flabberghast looked down and prodded the

sugar bowl, then glanced up at Nine through the green smoke. Nine stared back. *No life*, *no freedom*, *nothing…*

"Good," she said, still staring at the tin. "Bye, then." She stuffed the tin into her satchel, feeling for the jewel for the twentieth time and then began to march down the hallway.

"Oh and," she said over her shoulder, "you might like to take that skeleton out of the closet. Give him a dusting down, especially the ribs. I think he'd like that."

"Madam…" said Flabberghast in an uncomfortable voice. Nine paused, looking down at the plum carpet. "Thank you."

Nine didn't talk back, didn't look back. Down the hallway she only briefly paused at the portrait of Marcus the Disagreeable (1769–1835). She tipped the picture at a slight angle. It stayed there for half a second, then straightened itself up. She allowed herself a little smile.

Time to go. The brass door handle felt cool on her hand, which, for some odd reason, seemed to be sweating slightly.

Footsteps lolloped down the hallway. Nine ignored them and yanked opened the door. The rush of morning air greeted her. There was the alley. All the nonsense with the House was behind her. Soon it would be gone for ever.

Something pressed lightly into her left hand, then the footsteps thudded slowly away. Nine closed her eyes to try and shut out the wave of feelings. She didn't need to look at her hand to see what was there but, even so, she opened her eyes and glared at the boiled sweet, a million thoughts, feelings and arguments whirring around in her brain. But she couldn't – and wouldn't – look back. She fixed her eyes on the alley, jutted out her jaw and let her hand droop slightly so the sweet tumbled out onto the plum carpet. She had acquired what she came for. Now she could leave.

"Goodbye and good riddance," she murmured.

She raised her foot to take the step over the threshold. She was free. She was going to be finally … *free*.

She shut the front door behind her.

Nine didn't look over her shoulder as she marched on but with every step she took a single word shouted and shouted in her brain. It shouted as she passed the dilapidated library. It shouted as she passed the waking marketplace. And it shouted loudest of all as she stood outside the door of the pawn shop until she could no longer ignore it. The pawnbroker inside the shop flipped the door sign to 'OPEN'.

Nine reached inside her satchel and pulled out the oval sapphire. The word bellowed and bellowed in her brain and now a rising sense of panic came with it—

"Nine?" came a familiar voice behind her. "What *are* you doing?"

She whirled around, wide-eyed and tense, to look at Mr Downes. The librarian straightened his horn-rimmed spectacles and raised a gingery eyebrow. Nine took one last look at the sapphire, then grabbed his hand and slammed the jewel into it. "For the library. Repair it, buy new books. Especially mystery ones."

Mr Downes' eyes lit up and, for a moment, all his worry lines melted away. He stared at Nine. She hoped her eyes spoke back the words she couldn't say. She turned to go but he grabbed her arm. "But – wait – what *is* going on?"

Nine finally gave in to the thought – the word – that had been shouting in her brain. "Strawberries," she said before she ran, smiling at Mr Downes' loud, exasperated sigh behind her.

The House was, without question, the most ridiculous, most unbelievable, most irritating place she had ever known in her life, filled with the most ridiculous, most unbelievable and most irritating beings she had ever known in her life.

And she loved it.

Past the marketplace, the library, down the maze of alleys to the House. Relief hit her like a tide as she saw it was still there. She pounded on the front door and refused to smile at the look of delight on the troll's face. She had just one word for him.

"MOVE." She stepped inside, noticing the

225

chaotic clutter had been sucked back into the cupboard under the stairs.

The InkFree quill … the folded parchment in her satchel … the words she had written earlier as they had hurtled into her head… She took out the quill and parchment from her bag and scribbled down one final thought. She stepped out through the door one last time and propped the paper against the wall of the House, standing the purple tin of tea next to it.

"Goodbye," she murmured to the alley, "and good riddance."

She slammed the door shut and looked at the coat of arms where there was now a long, pink chain-like tongue poking out of the toad. She pulled it out, released it and—

ZA-BAM! Nine felt a shockwave rock through her body. But it wasn't enough to shake her smile.

EPILOGUE

The fishwife walked across the uneven cobbles, a basket full of dead, surprised-looking fish wobbling in the crook of her arm. With her free hand, she tightened the shawl around her head and neck as she headed for the back gate in the wall. Then she noticed a little purple tin and something flat and pale on the cobbles near the alley's end. She moved towards them, placed her basket on the ground and picked up the folded piece of parchment.

To Whoever Reads This Note,

My name is Nine and I need you to do me a favour.

Go down Whinney's Passage until you reach the tumbledown terrace. Knock on the third door and say, "No strawberries today".

Tell Pockets that Nine sent you. Tell the old weasel-faced devil he will never see me again. Why? Because he's wrong – sometimes life does bring you strawberries. Sometimes you are a whisper away from magic without even realising it.

And that's exactly what happened to me.

Nine

P.S. And tell him to drink this tea. It's just magical.

The fishwife put the tin in her basket and turned back down the alley to deliver the note and the tea.

"Consequences," she murmured, as she went. And underneath the scarlet shawl, the witch smiled.

Acknowledgements

Every story begins life as a magical spark, and there is a whole team of marvellous and enthusiastic people who fan it into a beautiful flame. I'm immensely grateful for everyone who has done this along the way, as otherwise this story would consist of nothing more than the words "*The House at the Edge of Magic –* fun idea?" in a star-speckled notebook. (And that's a bit short for a book).

So firstly, a huge sparkly thanks to my wonderful agent, Julia Churchill, who always believed in this story, even when the first draft resembled the Cupboard Under the Stairs.

Thank you for your patience, your enthusiasm and for laughing in all the right places. I most definitely owe you a potful of The Finest Tea in All the Realms.

A big heartfelt thank you to everyone at Walker for totally understanding and loving Nine and wanting to share her story. Special thanks to Denise Johnstone-Burt for falling in love with the title, the House and the world; to my extremely talented editor, Gráinne Clear, for a phenomenal job in keeping an excitable author and her gaggle of unruly characters under control (more or less); and to the absolutely spot-on Non Pratt, who pointed out there are only so many times a person should flop into a chair. You have all sprinkled magic of your own into this book. Thank you.

Books are always brought to life with pictures, and I'm delighted to be working with the amazing Ben Mantle. Thank you so much, Ben, for capturing these characters and their world so perfectly. An absolutely stunning job.

Huge thanks to my mum/Official Sounding-Board for loving these characters and hearing their voices as loudly as I do. (They move to her head when they give up trying to get through to me). And thanks to my dad for encouraging me to write for older children in the first place, and for keeping and treasuring all the things I wrote when I was a child. It is such a gift to know that someone believes in you. A special thumbs-up to you both for bravely entertaining a large handful of your grandchildren while I escaped to a café to create the Sometimes Dead. As you do.

I must give a shout out to librarians everywhere who open so many doors and possibilities to children, helping them to discover other worlds. Most of my own magical adventures were because of you. Thank you.

And finally, to my husband Alyn and our six children. It's not always easy having a wife and mother who spends a significant portion of her time in a completely different reality, balancing wooden spoons on her shoulder and muttering about evil toilets. Thank you for putting up with me (and the host of characters which regularly and inevitably burst into our lives and set up home). Here's to many more magical adventures with you all. Hopefully without the evil toilets...

About the Author

Amy Sparkes studied English Literature and Theology at the University of Kent, and began writing after moving to Devon with her husband, six young children and an overactive imagination. Her books have appeared on CBeebies storytime and been shortlisted for several book awards, including the Roald Dahl Funny Prize and the BookTrust Best Books Awards for *Do Not Enter the Monster Zoo*. She runs author events for children, writing workshops for aspiring children's writers, produces the Writing for Children pages for bestselling *Writing Magazine*, and writes short stories for *Aquila* magazine. She co-founded the Writing Magazine Picture Book Prize for aspiring picture book authors.

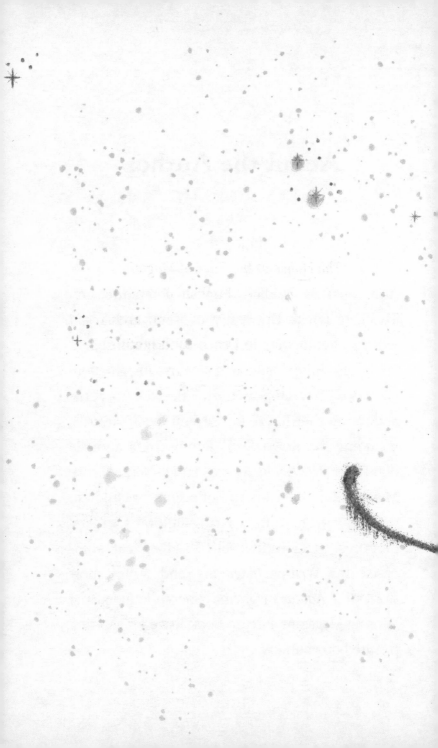

Enjoyed
The House at the Edge of Magic?

There'll be more from Nine, Flabberghast,
Eric and Spoon in their next adventure.

Coming soon...

We'd love to hear what you thought of
The House at the Edge of Magic!

🐦 #HouseAtTheEdge
@WalkerBooksUK
@AmySparkes

📷 @WalkerBooksUK